G000021732

Stowaway

Book Four of The Gifted Series

By Ana Ban

Stowaway by Ana Ban

© 2018   Ana Ban. All rights reserved.

No part of this book may be reproduced in any written, electronic, recording, or photocopying without written permission of the publisher or author. The exception would be in the case of brief quotations embodied in the critical articles or reviews and pages where permission is specifically granted by the publisher or author.

The author can be reached through Facebook @anabannovels

Although every precaution has been taken to verify the accuracy of the information contained herein, the author and publisher assume no responsibility for any errors or omissions. No liability is assumed for damages that may result from the use of information contained within.

All Persons Fictitious Disclaimer:
This book is a work of fiction. Any similarity between the characters and situations within its pages and places or persons, living or dead, is unintentional and coincidental.

1.Romance 2.Fantasy 3.Paranormal

First Edition

Printed in the USA

ISBN 9781980558422

This book is dedicated to Katie, one of my favorite redheads.
Your quick wit and capacity to care never ceases to amaze me.

Contents

The Elemental Family Tree

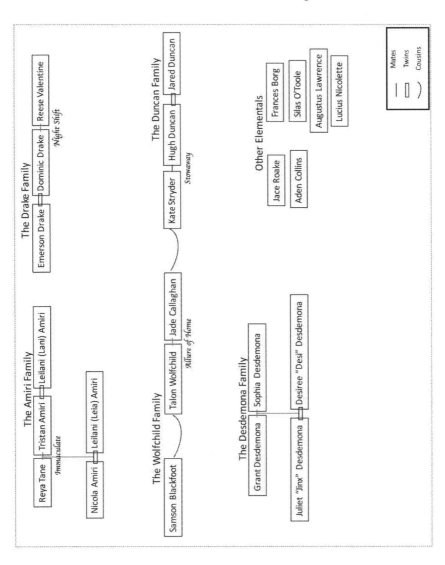

Prologue

Hugh

In the dark of night, feet pounded against the pavement. Light glaring from above chased me from the shadows, throwing me from the cover of trees and stumbling into a paved lot.

The soft *whoompa whoompa* from nearby helicopter blades echoed against my skull, urging me forward. Desperate for a place to hide, I began lifting door handles on parked cars, praying for just one to be open. A crowd of people exited the nearby restaurant, and my search became frantic.

Finally, an open door. Pulling myself inside the large SUV, I hauled myself over the backseat and into the trunk, landing on several duffle bags packed full.

I'd lost too much blood and needed to feed. Thirst was my only thought, front and center. I was weak, I was beaten, and I was running from...

The thought sent a spear of pain through my mind and I grabbed at my hair with both hands, holding back a scream. Panting, I forced myself to think of my thirst. It was the only thing that didn't trigger the crushing pain.

My name... who I was... it was all a blank. Where I was, why I'd been in that facility in the first place... blackness threatened to take over once again, as I couldn't stop wondering at what I'd lost.

Struggling to remain conscious, a sound finally broke through. Light, melodious laughter. The voice settled into my lungs like a breath of fresh air, a siren's call so beautiful and so... familiar.

Suddenly, I felt safe. Suddenly, I could let go.

Allowing the darkness to take over, for the first time in days, I slept.

Chapter 1

Kate

Wㅤhat about the time old man Rogers found spiders in his desk?"

"They were non-poisonous," I defended myself.

"My favorite was when you held the marlin for ransom," piped in Susie, my closest friend from work.

"We all got donuts, didn't we?" I answered.

This was my going away party. Though I'd been born and raised in Boston, and had been lucky enough to get hired onto Nelson and Sons fresh out of college, I had been head hunted by a company in California. I couldn't pass up the opportunity- or the sunshine.

As my coworkers continued to reminisce about my antics over the years, I found my attention drifting. It wasn't because I was nervous about the move- to be perfectly honest, while I enjoyed the company of the people surrounding me, Boston had stopped being home without my mom.

Now, even my happiest memories were shrouded in a melancholy haze.

No, something else was at play here, but I couldn't place what was wrong. It was just a nagging feeling in the pit of my stomach.

I was ready to be on my way.

Finally able to bow out gracefully, I was followed to my car by the most die-hard of the group.

"Knock 'em dead, Kate!"

Laughing at the well wishes, I made it to my door before being stopped.

"You don't have to leave tonight," said Marc, a second-year intern at the firm.

He was cute in the typical jock way, and had made subtle advances toward me in the past. He was a nice enough guy, but I just wasn't interested in him.

Or anyone.

"I'm a night owl anyway," I reminded him for the hundredth time.

"But if you stay, you could spend the night with me."

Stilling completely, I turned to fully face him. Though I didn't want to hurt his feelings, I did want to be firm.

"You know if I do that, I'll never leave," I winked. "It's best to part as friends."

He gave me a sloppy smile, then leaned in to kiss me on the cheek.

"Good luck, Red," he said, using the nickname that had become popular around the office.

"Thanks, buddy. I'll let you all know when I make it."

Escaping into my car, I let out a breath. As I began to pull away from the restaurant, I felt my nerves settle and the nagging feeling disappear.

I was where I should be.

∞ ∞ ∞

*T*he gas tank was full and I had enough songs on my playlist to not repeat for three full days. It was more than enough to keep me company on the cross-country trek.

As I sped down the highway, I sang loudly and with little talent. When I crossed the Boston city limits, I didn't even look back.

I drove for a solid four hours before deciding it was time for a pitstop. Pulling into a gas station, I refilled and, noticing some sketchy looking figures in the shadows, locked my doors as I went inside. After using the restroom, I filled up the largest cup of coffee they offered- loading it with cream and sugar- grabbed some snacks, and headed back to my car.

The figures I'd spotted earlier were gone. Shrugging it off, I put my car in gear and jumped back onto the highway.

The night was long, but it had always been my time. Even as a child, I preferred staying up late, practically lost in my own little world. The night was quiet, and it was beautiful.

As a marketing strategist, I did consulting work and could make my own hours. As long as I got the job done, and met with who I needed to meet with on their time table, I had the freedom to choose. I already knew I would use that to my advantage, working into the night and sleeping the afternoon away, as I preferred.

It was summer, but the heat wasn't sweltering. I enjoyed the seemingly endless forests of the eastern United States, and kept a sharp eye out for deer or other wild animals. For this first leg of the journey, I was hoping to make it to Cleveland before exhaustion took over. Instead of heading straight to San Francisco, I was making a somewhat out-of-the-way stop in a small town of Minnesota, right on the western edge of Lake Superior. In order to make it there, I decided to drive through Chicago. I would find a hotel just outside the city, or even make my way up into Madison before stopping for my second day. That way, I'd arrive in Duluth early enough to visit with family.

About an hour after crossing into Pennsylvania, I began to smell the unmistakable scent of ragweed. The road was dark; no streetlights and not a car to be seen, and the allergy-causing plant grew in abundance along the edge of the road. Another town was approaching, and I looked forward to having a small reprieve from the utter darkness.

Though I wasn't allergic to ragweed, or anything else, for that matter, I wasn't completely immune to its effects. My nose began to itch, and I was even more anxious now to arrive in a town, where the plants wouldn't be growing in such abundance.

As I began to see the first vestiges of humanity, a sound resounded throughout the tight confines of the SUV, causing me to jerk the wheel and screech in fear.

"*Aa-choo!*"

"What the hell!" I yelled, my head whipping around to search the interior of the car as my foot slammed instinctively on the brake.

"Wait, please," a low, husky voice pleaded with me from the trunk.

My heart thudding like taiko drums, I looked into the rearview mirror where a pair of eyes stared back at me. They were the deepest brown, like the color of earth after it rains. Tortured even in the dim light, they clung to me as if I was a lifeline.

Our gazes snagged and held, and I felt like the very deer I was in constant search of. Frozen, mesmerized by the light shining back at me.

"Please, don't be afraid," the voice spoke again. "I'm not going to hurt you. I'm... injured..."

Those fathomless pools of desperation disappeared, and I heard a quiet *thunk* as the stranger landed on my bags.

Momentarily released from the spell, I took several quick breaths, realizing I was close to hyperventilating. There was a man, *in my trunk.* I was stopped dead in the middle of the highway, and I couldn't breathe.

Oddly, I felt no ill will from the stranger. On the contrary, every fiber of my being was screaming at me to help him.

Shaking my head, I attempted to assimilate the events over the last few moments with logic, and failed.

I had to do something. Sitting in the middle of the highway wishing for a paper bag to breathe into wasn't helping anyone.

"Who... who are you?" I managed, slowly beginning to move forward again.

But before he could respond, the familiar flash of blue and red lights lit up the night.

Chapter 2

error seizing me, I quickly sorted through my options. The man's head struggled to lift above the back seats, his own fear swamping me in the confines of the car.

"Please..." his voice was strangled, and I closed my eyes for the briefest moment.

Even behind my lids, the stranger's face remained.

Though I didn't know it, the next decision I made was the most important one I would *ever* make.

"Get into the backseat," I ordered the man, slowing the vehicle once again. "Buckle in, but close your eyes and pretend you're asleep."

Without questioning me, he moved quickly, though I could clearly tell it was taking a toll. When he slumped into the seat, I gasped as I took in his clothing.

They were dirty and blood streaked, his face even paler as the light faded from blue to red and back again.

For the briefest moment I questioned my own sanity, then managed to ask, "Is that your blood?"

"Yes," came the weak reply.

Letting out the breath I was holding, I stopped the vehicle completely.   Reaching over and grabbing a blanket from the passenger seat, I tossed it carefully back to him.

"Cover up.   Remember the seat belt.   Pretend you're sleeping."

While he followed my direction, I took several quick breaths to steady myself, willing the hand on the steering wheel to cease shaking.   In the rearview mirror, I watched those surprisingly arresting eyes slip closed.

There was a light tapping on the window, and I jumped. Chastising myself for being caught off guard, I rolled the window down and pasted a sheepish smile on my face.

"Hello, officer," I said, deceptively lightly.

"Evening, ma'am. Is everything all right? You swerved a bit back there."

"Oh, I'm so sorry," I told him. "There was a deer, and I know I'm not supposed to swerve but it was instinct."

The kind-looking officer nodded, then switched his flashlight toward the man in my backseat.

"That's my fiancé," I lied. "We're taking turns driving, and I swear he can sleep through anything."

Surreptitiously I crossed my fingers, praying the officer would buy my story.   I had another trick up my sleeve, but would rather resolve this the old-fashioned way.

By lying.

"He looks pretty tuckered out," the officer acknowledged. "Might be time for you both to stop and get some rest."

Nodding sagely, I agreed, "Sounds like a good idea, after that scare. I have a hotel mapped out two towns from now."

"All right missy, you drive carefully now. No ticket tonight."

"Thank you, sir," I smiled at him, relief flooding through me.

As soon as he was away from my vehicle, I sighed, flipped on my signal, and headed back onto the highway.

"You didn't have to do that," the man's voice was just a whisper of sound, and full of gratitude. "Thank you."

"I hope it was the right thing," I muttered, then risked a glance back at him. His eyes were open and watching me curiously. "What's your name?"

He started, his eyes first going wide, then narrowing into slits. Pain streaked across his features, and I fumbled with what to do.

"I don't know," he finally responded in a hoarse whisper.

"You need a hospital," I chided, angry with myself for not thinking of that first.

"No," he answered firmly. "No hospitals."

"You're bleeding!" I practically yelled. Calming myself, I tried to force him to see reason. "You're obviously in trouble, and bleeding to death won't help you at all."

There was a slight twitch along his lips, and I thought he wanted to smile.

"I need blood," his voice was barely above a whisper now. "No hospitals."

As I was about to question this, his eyes slid closed again. With no small amount of effort, he forced out his repeated request.

"Please... no... hos... tals."

Switching my gaze forward, I thought through my options. A hospital should have been my first and only thought, but there was something about this man. Something that made me believe him, and I knew I would do everything in my power to help him.

But who's going to help me?

∞　∞　∞

 hough I hadn't planned on stopping so soon, the state of the stranger in my backseat was worrisome. I found a motel on the edge of the next town with a vacancy sign, so I pulled in to grab a room. Running inside the small office, I booked a room and asked for extra towels, any type of first aid they had, and a sewing kit.

Moving the SUV directly in front of the room I'd been given, I propped open the door before hurrying to the back of the car. When I opened the back door, the man slumped toward me.

Catching him, I examined his face for a moment, slack now in sleep. It was difficult to determine his age, though I would think he wasn't much older than my 29 years. His broad shoulders were deceptively muscular, I thought erratically as I unbuckled and attempted to grip him around the waist.

"Come on, help me out a little," I pleaded.

He seemed to come out of his stupor for just a few moments, enough to lend me what little strength he had. Between the two of us, we got him inside and lying atop one of the beds.

Not wasting any time, I hurried back out to the car to grab the items I'd acquired from the office, along with my overnight bag.

Shutting and locking the door, I stepped up to the strange man that was now in my care. Sitting carefully on the edge of the bed, I pushed his overgrown hair from his eyes. He was asleep again, or perhaps even just unconscious from pain- it was difficult to tell.

With shaking hands, I began to peel off the man's jacket and shirt, wincing as the cloth stuck to his wounds. When his stomach and chest were revealed, I let out a gasp of shock.

Every inch of skin was marked in crisscrossed wounds. These were not as deep as the gouges along his lower stomach, where the majority of the blood had come from, but horrible just the same

Who would have done this?

More importantly for the moment, who could have survived such a thing?

This man was not just in trouble. This man had been *tortured*.

Steeling myself for the task ahead, I scrounged through my own bag and found a large Tupperware bowl filled with trail mix. Dumping the contents out, I filled the container with warm, soapy water. Sitting beside the man again, I carefully washed off all the dried blood. There was so much I needed to refill my makeshift water basin several times.

There were hundreds of thoughts racing through my mind, and I did my best to push them aside for the time being. It did no good to stress about questions that had no answer. And from what I saw earlier, it didn't seem the stranger would be able to provide any information either, even if he'd been conscious.

Did he have amnesia, then? Where did he come from? He must have climbed into my trunk sometime between me packing up the bags and discovering him when he sneezed. His voice carried a slight accent, though it wasn't overly obvious and therefore difficult for me to pinpoint.

Once the dried blood was cleared, I used a hefty amount of antiseptic, grateful for his unconscious state as the wounds popped and sizzled under the liquid's affect.

There was one deep gash that had me worrying my lower lip; the rest would heal on their own, but this one needed help. Every year, we were required to take a first aid course at work; so, while I understood the concept of stitches, I'd never actually had the need to practice my skill.

"No time like the present," I spoke aloud, grabbing the small sewing kit before I could change my mind.

First dragging the bed lamp as close as I was able, I then chose black thread and strung it through the smallest needle before dipping it all in the antiseptic. With a steadying breath, I bent to the task before me.

"It's just fabric," I told myself. "It's just fabric."

Refusing to focus on the fact that I was stabbing through human skin, I made surprisingly quick work of closing the wound. Snipping off the excess thread, I sat straight and let out a sigh. Digging through the small box of first aid, I found four Band-Aids, which I used to cover parts of the stitch site. It looked like something a 3-year-old would do while playing doctor.

"You better be worth it," I smirked at my patient, needing a moment of levity.

Then, with a sigh, I began to clean up.

His shirt was ruined, though I attempted to wash it out in the sink. Giving up, I stuck it in a plastic bag and set it next to my duffel bag to throw in a dumpster later. I wouldn't be leaving a bloody shirt for housekeeping to find.

Digging through my bag, I found an extra sleep shirt- I preferred yoga pants and men's t-shirts for my pajamas- and brought the piece of clothing over. It would fit, but I didn't think I'd be able to dress him on my own, without aggravating his wounds. Tossing the shirt onto the bed, I grabbed a clean towel to lay across his chest instead, before pulling the blanket up.

Feeling his forehead, I frowned at his seemingly low temperature. A fever wouldn't have surprised me, but this chill... it was odd, to say the least.

Of course, what *wasn't* odd about this situation?

Grabbing the bedspread from the second bed, along with an extra blanket that was kept in the closet, I piled those on as well. I stood, hands on hips, staring at the stranger who had disrupted my entire life in a matter of moments.

Now that I could focus on the man instead of the injuries, my eyes traced along the sharp jaw and hard lines of a face that had quite obviously seen too much in his short life. There was a light scruff along his jaw and dark, arched brows over what I knew to be intense eyes. Watching him, I felt a strange stirring low in my stomach. At first, I didn't recognize what the almost queasy feeling was, but then it hit me: I was attracted to him.

That was crazy. Yes, he had a handsome face, but I wasn't attracted to *anyone*. For a long time, I thought perhaps there was something wrong with me; as I grew older and realized I had my own goals and interests, the opposite sex had become lower and lower in my priorities.

Yet here, completely out of the blue, a man that I was attracted to has fallen into my lap.

Or, more specifically, my SUV.

Needing a few moments to myself, I backed away and thought through my options.

He seemed to be down for the count, and I felt grungy from the day- my last day of work in Boston, the dinner with my coworkers, the hours driving and playing doctor had all taken their toll.

Though I didn't like the idea of leaving the man unattended, I decided a hot shower was worth the risk.

Grabbing my toiletries, I turned the knob as hot as it would go, allowing the steam to fill up the small space. Debating on the door, I decided to leave it open. In case the man woke and needed help, I would be able to hear him.

Without further thought, I stripped off my clothes and allowed the water to slough away the grime of the day.

Chapter 3

Though I wanted to soak in the heat, I kept the shower quick. Wrapping myself in a towel, I poked my head around the corner to check on my patient. He was still asleep, blankets piled high.

Choosing to clean his wounds myself was insane, and while I acknowledged that thought, I also dismissed it. Clearly, this man was in trouble; the kind of trouble the police wouldn't be able to assist with. There was something in his eyes that made me trust him, and now that I'd made that decision, I was going the distance.

Even if that meant the addition of a driving buddy who was, even in his injured and unconscious state, undeniably sexy.

I dressed quickly, leaving a towel wrapped around my long, vibrantly red hair. Sinking onto the edge of the second bed, I watched the stranger for a while.

"I need something to call you," I announced to the room. "You look like a superhero to me. Dark and mysterious. Muscly. And tortured."

Wincing at the word that popped out of my mouth, I quickly moved on.

"That pretty much describes Batman. And, come to think of it, I've never seen you and Batman in the same room at the same time."

Standing, I moved closer to the bed, reaching out to brush away that same chunk of hair from his eyes.

"You hear me, Batman? You *will* survive this. I'm going to make sure of it."

"I'm working on it," the man responded, his lips barely moving.

Startled, I brought my hand up to my chest, hugging it there.

"You're awake?" I asked.

"Yes," he responded, then slowly lifted his lashes.

When his eyes met mine, I felt that same strange, liquid feeling, though now it spread down to my toes.

"Thank you," he murmured. Then, squinting up at me as if he were having difficulty seeing, he asked, "What happened to your hair?"

Automatically my hand lifted to touch my hair and encountered the towel still twisted around the mass. Chuckling, I made quick work of releasing the long mane.

"I was letting it dry," I explained, as the bright red chunks fell across my shoulders.

"It's the color of a kakabeak flower," he said on a breath, his hand rising weakly to touch the tips of my hair softly. "My favorite flower."

Shock held me still as he drifted back into sleep. What in the world was a kakabeak flower?

After making sure he was comfortable, I dug out my cell phone. It was 3:00 in the morning, and I was exhausted. For a brief moment I considered calling someone– a family member, or the police– but ultimately decided against it. This man had sparked something in me, and it was more than the startling realization that I was attracted to him. I felt *protective* of him.

Crossing my legs under me and leaning against the pillows, I pulled up the internet on my phone and made my best attempt to spell kakabeak. Tapping on images, I found an array of an interestingly beautiful flower, unlike anything I'd ever seen. It hung down off branches, opening in long, red petals. Each petal was thick and hardy, and I found myself enjoying the comparison.

Curious about its origins, I clicked on an article to find the flower was indigenous to New Zealand, and endangered. That was sad, but it gave me some information, at least.

Glancing over at Batman thoughtfully, I wondered if New Zealand was his home. That could be the slight accent I was picking up when he spoke, though he had obviously worked on an American accent. It gave us a starting place, at the very least. New Zealand wasn't *that* big, right?

Getting up again, I brushed through my hair, then turned out all lights but one, in case either of us woke in confusion. Then, I lay in the bed opposite my guest, and watched his dark form until sleep took me.

∞ ∞ ∞

$\mathcal{W}$ hen I woke, it was with complete disorientation. Bleary eyes squinted at my surroundings, attempting to piece together the nights' events with my current surroundings.

Oh, yeah. I was in a hotel room with a total stranger, who had been tortured.

Sitting up with a jerk, I planted my feet on the floor and focused on Batman's form. To my surprise, his eyes were open and steadily on me.

"Good morning," I said groggily. "How are you feeling?"

"Better," he responded, his voice gruff with sleep. Of course, he only sounded sexier while I sounded like a hag.

My groan at the thought must have been aloud, for he looked at me curiously.

"What is it?"

"Nothing," I answered quickly, rising from the bed. "Let me check your wounds."

"First, would you please tell me your name?"

With a grin, I answered him, "My name is Kate, Kate Stryder. Any luck on yours?"

I watched as pain flitted across his features, and immediately regretted asking.

"Don't worry about it. I'll just keep calling you Batman," I told him to lighten the mood.

Turning on the bedside lamp, I moved the pile of blankets aside. The towel was still in place, with dried blood spots. Wincing as I grasped the edge of the towel, knowing it wouldn't feel good if the fabric stuck to any of the wounds, I lifted as gently as I was able.

My eyes narrowed as his chest was revealed, and I began to pull the towel off quicker. Running a finger over the smooth surface of his ribs, I stared in confusion as my eyes drifted to my sewing job.

An angry red welt was the only sign of the contusion that had been deep enough to warrant stitches.

Switching my gaze from the non-existent wounds back to my patient's face, I found my jaw hanging open, unable to form words to match my thoughts.

"What is it?" he asked, his brows drawing together at my expression.

"Your wounds... they're healed," I finally let out.

"That's good news, is it not?" His hand reached up to cup my cheek, his thumb swiping gently under my eye. "Why do you seem so worried?"

"That's... that's not normal," I burst out, telling my body to take a step back but unable to move away from his touch.

Rescinding his hand, the man's expression morphed from confusion to worry. "I don't understand."

Once the contact with his palm released me from my trance, I sank down onto the bed beside him. Knowing I shouldn't be this close, given my unusual reaction to him, I still couldn't seem to find the energy to move.

"You had wounds all over your chest," I explained after sucking in a deep breath. "And one really deep one, that I had to stitch up."

Running a finger gently along the welt that was the only remaining visible injury, I watched as his body tensed. His breathing changed, and as my eyes met his, I realized just how intimate a gesture I had just performed.

"I'm so sorry," I began, but before I could move my hand away, he gripped my wrist with a strength that belied his prone position.

"Don't be sorry," he shook his head, his eyes never leaving mine. "It's just... your touch... your scent... I'm having strange reactions to you, and I don't understand anything that's happening."

Letting out a breath, I managed a small smile. "That makes two of us."

Glancing at the bedside clock, I realized it was just past 6:00. I'd only slept a few hours, but that wasn't unusual.

"Let me take the stitches out," I said, standing in search of scissors.

He waited patiently for me to return, watching my face as I concentrated on my task. With the skin knitted back together, the removal was easy.

Finally meeting his eye, I said the first thing I could think of.

"Are you hungry? I can get us something to eat," I offered.

"Yes... no," he amended, and grimaced. "I'm... thirsty."

Pointing toward the sink area, I began, "There's some cups, I can get you a water..."

"No," he interrupted me. "It's not water I need."

My eyes met his again, and I felt my heart give one pounding beat at the look in his. I didn't understand what he meant, but something told me I wouldn't enjoy finding out.

"What do you need?" I asked, my voice barely above a whisper.

"Blood," he answered softly. "I need blood."

"We could get you a transfusion at the hospital..." I trailed off as his expression registered. "You're not talking about a transfusion."

"Kate," he said my name with an emotion I couldn't quite place. "Please don't be afraid of me. I don't remember anything about myself, or who can help me. Right now, you are the only person I know, and the only person I can trust. Please believe me when I say I would do nothing to ever harm you."

Swallowing, I nodded once. Though I had a feeling I wouldn't like where this conversation was going, I couldn't deny the evidence in front of me. I knew, without a doubt, how bad that wound had been. And now, it was practically healed. There was something different about this man that was unlike anything I'd come across, and I would do my best to keep an open mind.

Besides, it wasn't like *I* was the most normal person in the world.

Taking a deep breath, I did my best to reassure him.

"I believe you," I told him. "We're in this together, whatever it is and whatever happens next. Just tell me what you need."

The relief pouring from his body was palpable.

"I need blood. To drink. It will help me regain my energy. But, I believe regular food will also assist with that."

"Can we get blood from a blood bank? Or do you... eat people?"

To my surprise, he cracked a smile.

"I am able to take blood from a human without harming them," he answered slowly, as if testing the information. "I don't believe I *eat people*, but just in case, I think a blood bag would be preferable."

Relief flooded through me, but a new problem presented itself.

"All right, but how do we get a blood bag?"

His gaze shifted to stare off at nothing while he thought this through. After a few moments, his eyes met mine again.

"You won't like this."

Sighing, I answered for him. "We're going to steal it, aren't we?"

Chapter 4

After discussing a few strategies, I left Batman to shower and ventured into town. Thank goodness for Walmart- I found all the supplies we needed, purchasing them quickly and doing a drive-by of the only hospital in town. Getting the general layout, I made it back to the motel to find my patient sitting on the edge of the bed, a remote in his hand.

His dark hair was damp from his shower, and his skin had a fresh, rosy glow. The jeans he wore hung low, his chest bare as his shirt had been ruined. After a moment of gawking, I cleared my throat and looked anywhere but the half-naked man in my room.

"What is this drivel?" he asked, staring at the screen. "Is this what passes for entertainment?"

Holding back a laugh, I dumped the bags on the bed and switched off the television.

"Enough of that." I told him. Picking up the shirt I'd discarded the night before, I tossed it in his lap. "Why don't you put this on? And then let's eat."

Pulling out several small containers from the deli department, I handed Batman a plastic fork before digging into a pasta salad. After taking a few bites, I switched to the next container- mashed potatoes- before realizing he hadn't begun eating.

"What's wrong?"

"This food is unfamiliar to me," he responded, poking at it with the utensil.

"It's mac and cheese," I told him. "Just try it, you'll like it, I promise."

I watched as Batman steeled himself before taking a delicate bite. The food moved around his mouth while he adjusted to the flavor.

"Surprisingly good," he announced after swallowing.

"Here, try this," I said, handing over the mashed potatoes, which were smothered in gravy. "One of my faves."

He accepted the container from me, then continued to try each item I'd bought.

"What do you remember before you ended up in my trunk?" I asked, scooping some fruit into my mouth.

"I was being held in a facility. I believe I was drugged- I woke very groggy, and with no memory. No one was guarding me when I came to, and I escaped. I was spotted on the way out, and I ran a long time through woods. Eventually I came to a parking lot... I remember being chased, and hearing helicopters above... but that's it. I knew they were close, and I started trying doors until one opened."

"You must have been near the restaurant," I murmured, mostly to myself. "It was on the outskirts of Boston, with a good chunk of woods nearby."

He nodded, then continued, "I woke when you stopped at a gas station. I was going to escape then, and leave you be, but you'd locked the doors. If I'd opened them from the inside, the alarm would have gone off, attracting more attention to me."

"I hardly ever lock my doors," I told him with a smirk. "But there were some shady looking people, and it was late. I guess it worked out for the best."

His eyes met mine, and I felt that curious tingle of awareness spreading across my stomach.

Clearing my throat, I picked up another container and ceased my questions for the time being.

Once we were satisfied, he announced his favorites were the mac and cheese, along with the buffalo wings.

Cleaning up our odd breakfast feast, I dragged out the scrubs I'd bought, handing him his outfit for the day. Our plan was to get into the hospital dressed as nurses, then go from there.

"I also got you some normal clothes," I told him, "since your shirt was ruined, and you'll need more things to wear. I guessed on your size, but we can always stop and get more if we need to."

"Thank you," he said, his eyes watching me carefully. "You've done so much for me already, and you must have your own life to get back to. If you need to leave me now, I will understand."

Though I should have jumped at the chance, the idea of leaving him gave me palpitations. Instead, I shrugged casually.

"Look, here's the deal: I'm driving cross-country anyway, and you can come with me. At least until your memory returns, you'll be far away from whoever it was that did this to you," I gestured vaguely at his chest. "Unless you have another plan?"

"I don't. Thank you, Kate," he shook his head, attempting to hide his frustration at the situation. "Shall I change first, or would you like to?"

"I will," I responded.

Heading for the small bathroom, I pulled on the scrub outfit quickly. Just outside the bathroom was the sink with a mirror, and I used that to pull my hair back while Batman changed.

Once he emerged, we packed up all our belongings, including the bag containing his bloody clothes, and loaded my car. He seemed to be moving easier, though I could still see winces of pain occasionally.

"Are you sure you're up for this? We can rest for another day," I told him.

"I'll be fine," he assured me.

He made himself comfortable in the passenger seat while I started the car.

"Tell me more about yourself," he insisted as I began the drive.

"I was born and raised in Boston," I told him. "It was just me and my mom. Went to Boston University, and I've been working at Nelson and Son since I graduated. A few months ago, I was headhunted for a position in California, and I took it."

"You don't have a boyfriend, husband?"

I risked a glance over at him at this, as I felt the question was more than it seemed. He was looking steadfastly forward, his body stiff.

"Dating hasn't been a high priority for me," I responded, noticing his shoulders relax at the information. "And my mom... she passed away last year."

"I'm so sorry," he reached across to grip my hand in his.

The contact shocked me, but not just because it was unexpected. His skin was hot, almost feverish.

Night and day to the chilly temperature last night.

Concern instantly colored my tone. "Are you sure you're feeling okay? You're burning up."

"I feel fine," he replied, taking his hand back. "I think this may be normal."

Casting him a sideways glance, I considered my options. We could call this whole thing off, but I had a feeling that would be the worst thing we could do.

The problem was, I was completely out of my depth here, and I was already going against logic in helping him. Yet, I continued, driven by some unseen force that was beyond my understanding.

We drove the rest of the way in silence, and as I pulled into the parking lot across the street from the hospital, I took a deep breath before turning toward him.

"Blood bank is on the third floor," I told him. "We'll walk there together, then split up. While I distract the front desk, it'll be up to you to get into the secure area. Are you certain you can do this?"

He let out a breath. "I have no choice."

"It's 8:05 now," I commented. "We meet back here at 8:20, whether or not we're successful. Got it?"

Realizing he didn't have a way to tell time, I quickly slipped off my watch and clasped it on his wrist before sliding my phone into my pocket.

"Let's go!" I said with more enthusiasm than I was feeling.

We walked together at a quick pace, strolling through the sliding doors and pausing at a bank of elevators. Pressing the button for level three, I studied the panel listing each level before sneaking a glance at my new partner in crime.

Literally.

We were lucky in that the hospital held a blood donation center, which would have coolers of blood bags waiting to be transferred. Most hospitals didn't- they relied on outside business to collect and the Red Cross to deliver as needed.

I felt bad that we would be taking anything at all from a hospital, but I vowed to donate to them anonymously at a later date.

Checking the time as the doors opened, I reminded Batman, "Twelve minutes."

He nodded, flashing me the hint of a smile, before taking off in an opposite direction. I headed straight forward, to the reception desk.

There was one female nurse behind the desk, and a waiting room to the left. A doorway led to the donation area, while down the hall, where Batman had gone, was an "employee only" door that, I hoped, led to the coolers.

In my experience, the only time an employee would be in the back room was when they were bringing a new donation in. There would be two or three small rooms to do the initial screening tests to make sure a person qualified to make a donation, and then the larger room where the donations were drawn.

I just needed to make a big enough distraction that would bring any of the workers' attentions to me. As an idea struck, I held back a smirk and started walking.

Approaching the desk, I gave the nurse a bright smile before speaking in a rush.

"Hi, I'm from floor *nine*," I emphasized the level, as that was where the psych ward was located. "We've had a little... incident, and I was hoping I could ask everyone if they'd seen anyone wandering around down here that wasn't supposed to be."

"Oh, dear," the nurse sputtered. "I didn't receive any announcements..."

"We're trying to keep this low key," I told her hastily. "You see, the man thinks he's a... vampire."

The nurse stared at me with wide eyes, finally letting out a small, hiccupping laugh.

"I know, but there's a reason he's up there. The thing is, we think he came here, to... you know... get blood."

"Well, I suppose that's better than biting people," the nurse replied good naturedly. Then, she spoke into an earpiece, which I assumed connected everyone on the level. "We have a lost lamb, has anyone seen a level nine patient?"

While I couldn't hear the reply, I was watching the nurse's expression as the other worker's spoke.

"No one has seen anything," she shrugged at me. "But I'll keep an eye out."

"Great, thank you!" I replied, and, before she could ask my name or any other details, I spun on my heel and marched toward the elevators.

Batman was nowhere to be seen, but I had high hopes he'd accomplished his task.

As I exited the building, I practically ran back to the relative safety of my SUV. Opening the trunk, I popped open the lid of the cooler I'd bought that morning, which plugged into an outlet to keep items cold. Crossing an arm over my stomach, I propped my elbow up so I could chew on a nail, my mind racing through every negative possibility.

Just as the clock hit 8:20, the front door slammed closed, making me jump.

Batman was back, and he was in the front seat.

Letting out a breath of air, I asked, "Did you get what you need?"

He climbed over the console and into the backseat, untucking his shirt and shifting the bags of blood into the cooler.

"This will tide me over for a while. Thank you."

"Do you need one now?" I asked, hesitant with the question. Part of me was brimming with curiosity, while the majority of me was grossed out.

"No. I've already had some," he responded, looking away. Almost as if he were shy.

"Oh, okay. Great," I responded, tamping down the odd feeling of disappointment.

Closing the trunk, I hurried back to the front seat. He'd already climbed back into the passenger area, and I wasted no time in leaving the lot.

"That was smart, the story about the mental patient," Batman said suddenly. "Had they caught me, we would have been able to walk out. Also, once they find the missing bags, they'll blame it on someone mentally unstable."

Staring over at him, I asked the obvious, "How did you know that?"

He shifted uncomfortably, refusing to meet my eye. At first, I wasn't sure he was going to answer, but he finally spoke quietly.

"I could hear you."

Looking back to the road, my jaw worked for a moment before forming speech. "How?"

He let out a long sigh, and it was obvious he was as disturbed by this as I was about to be.

"There are some things I discovered, once I was infused with blood," he began. "I have exceptional hearing, for one."

"And?"

He was silent, so I asked again.

"And? What else?"

"I'm very fast. And strong."

Suddenly, the fact that he appeared in my front seat without my noticing made sense.

Jerking the car toward an exit, I picked up speed down the short side street before slamming the brakes.

Batman had one hand braced against the door, his face a mask of worry.

"What are you doing? Kate? Are you all right?"

"Prove it," I told him, pushing open the door and stalking to the front of the hood.

He followed me out, standing uncertainly a few feet away. "What do you mean?"

I'd stopped at a rest area; spread out before us was a large grassy area with picnic tables that gave way to a stand of trees. There were no other cars using the facilities, and the only cameras were positioned at the small building which housed the restrooms.

"Show me how fast you are," I prompted, gesturing toward the expanse of grass.

He hesitated a moment longer, then, right before my eyes, he disappeared.

Chapter 5

A split second after he'd disappeared, Batman returned, suddenly on my left side, holding out a wildflower.

Breathless, I looked between him and the edge of the trees, where I could make out a crop of the flowers.

Reaching out with shaking fingers, I accepted the delicate bud he'd picked for me.

"Whoa," I gasped, meeting his eye. "What *are* you?"

Realizing how rude that sounded, I wanted to take the words back but was unable.

His face fell, his gaze switching from my face to focus off to the horizon.

"I don't know," he whispered his answer.

"Hey, I'm sorry," I tried to soothe him.

Wrapping my fingers around his arm, I waited for him to look at me once more. He glanced down at my hand, surprised at the contact.

"I didn't mean it like that," I assured him. "It's just... wow. This is all new to me."

With a self-deprecating smile, he answered, "Me, too."

Casually, he moved his arm up and clasped his hot hand around mine. It was a soothing gesture, though I wasn't sure if it was meant for me or him.

Perhaps both.

His eyes bore into mine, and I searched the dark hue, enjoying the honeyed tints the morning sun coaxed out. The air between us became thick, and I sucked in a breath. Though neither of us seemed to move, we were suddenly closer. His lips were just a hairsbreadth from mine.

My tongue darted out, my own lips suddenly parched. His eyes tracked the movement, the hooded look insanely attractive. Still, we inched closer, moving toward the inevitable.

The fact that I had only just met this man, in the most unconventional way, *yesterday*, made no difference. The fact that we'd just stolen, from a hospital no less, made no difference. The fact that he drank blood, had incredible power and no sense of his past– none of it mattered.

The only thing that mattered was how his lips would feel when they finally touched mine.

Lifting onto my toes, I closed the gap, hesitant as our lips first touched. As inexperienced as I was, I didn't even know where to go from here. Luckily, some primitive need rose between us, and doubt flew out the window.

His arms, deceptively strong, wrapped around my waist. My own wound around his neck, the hand not holding the flower sinking into his thick hair. We were pressed so closely together I could barely breathe, yet I wanted more. I pushed myself into his body, and he pushed back until I was trapped against the hood of my car. His head dipped to kiss along my neck before rising again, his tongue delving deep and tangling with my own.

The temperature rose around me until I was sure I would see steam when I finally opened my eyes. My blood sang in my veins. Reached toward him. Begging to be...

With a gasp I pushed away, panting with the effort. He looked just as dazed as I felt, his eyes slowly adjusting on mine.

I shook with the impact of our kiss, and the thought that I had so quickly cut off.

I'd wanted him to drink my blood.

Only one thing could distract me from that terrifying thought.

He took a deep, shuddering breath before speaking in a hollow whisper.

"I... I remember my name."

Shock registered on his face, reflecting on my own. I didn't breathe, couldn't think past the moment. When he spoke again, his voice came out sure, strong. Relieved.

"It's Hugh. My name is Hugh."

The relief Hugh felt at remembering his own name was tangible. It was a relief for me, too. Especially since I'd just kissed a man, and I didn't even know his name.

"Hugh," I said, testing it out. "Doesn't have the same ring as Batman, but it'll do."

We shared a grin, the sudden mood shift doing a lot to settle my nerves.

"Do you remember anything else?"

"No," he answered, though it didn't diminish his mood. "But, it's a start."

"That it is," I responded.

There was an awkward silence as we both struggled with a way to bring up the intense moment we'd just shared.

"About earlier…" I began, and he reached out to cup my cheek with his hand.

"That was incredible," he said, his tone as serious as I'd ever heard it. "And I would like to explore this connection we have, but I know it's not fair to you. None of this is."

That hadn't been what I was expecting. My initial reaction was to deny his claim.

"Why do you say that?"

Dropping his hand, he replied, "I remember nothing of my past, besides the place I escaped from. Every moment I'm with you I put you in harm's way. I have powers I still know nothing about."

"Oh, well, that," I answered, forcing out a chuckle. "Look, this is crazy, but… I've never responded to someone like that before. There's a reason you picked my car to climb into, and a reason I chose to help you even though it defied all logic."

Stepping close, I placed a hand against his chest, watching his eyes with mine.

"I'm in this with you. Wherever it may lead."

His eyes softened at my admission, his palm brushing against my cheek again. Gently, he pulled me closer, leaving a soft kiss against my lips.

"Then, we do this. Together."

Wanting to prolong the moment, I dropped my head to rest against his chest. Though I was by no means short at 5'8, Hugh still towered over me. His arms wrapped around my waist, and I answered in kind. For several long moments we stood in the deserted park, holding onto each other in a world gone mad.

Eventually, in unspoken understanding, we drew apart to get back into the SUV. Settling into the drive, I jumped in surprise when Hugh took my free hand in his, though I didn't pull away. The contact with his hot skin was comforting, and oddly familiar.

"Tell me more about your family," Hugh prompted once we were underway.

Keeping my eyes on the road, I began to tell him my story.

"Well, I told you earlier it was just me and my mom while I was growing up. I didn't meet my dad until a little over a year ago. He and my mom had a fling back when they were in college, and by the time she realized she was pregnant, he had already moved back to Minnesota, where the rest of his– where the rest of *my* family is from."

I paused here, keeping my emotions in check.

"My mom decided to keep it to herself, since my dad had already moved on and had a promising career in law."

"Wouldn't he have wanted to know?" Hugh asked quietly.

"I think he would have moved back to be with her, with us. But, she didn't want him to make that choice. When she got sick, she came to regret keeping him away from me, and set up a meeting. He flew out to Boston for a week, and I've been to visit him also. Actually, my second visit was for a family reunion."

Here I turned to him, my eyes wide.

"*Hundreds* of people were there," I told him, still amazed at the event I'd been suckered into attending. "It was held in this tiny town in Wisconsin, and I met the entire extended family. Turns out I have some pretty cool cousins, and we've stayed in contact since then. I'd planned on stopping in Duluth, where my dad is living now, and two of my cousins are driving in to visit while I'm there."

"You said you'd *planned* on stopping- has that changed?" Hugh asked.

"Yeah, I just... I didn't know if you'd want to go with."

Hugh squeezed my hand with gentle, reassuring pressure. "Of course we will stop to see your family. I don't know what my future holds, but there is no doubt in my mind that you are a large part of it."

My reaction to his words was unexpected. My throat clogged, and I felt hot tears brimming. Sucking in a breath, I forced myself away from the tangle of emotions his sentiment produced.

"Kate? Are you all right?"

Unable yet to speak, I gave him a sharp nod.

"I'm sorry," Hugh lamented. "I shouldn't have said that. You don't feel the same."

"It's not that," I assured him, the emotion thick in my voice. Though it was embarrassing, I also didn't want him to believe I was rejecting him. "It's just... this has all happened so fast. I've never had feelings for anyone before, and I'm not really sure how to deal with them."

"And you barely know me. I barely know myself," he added, a note of sadness in his voice. "Though I can't say for certain, I don't believe I've ever felt this connection to anyone before, either."

"Then there's... what you're capable of," I continued. "I mean, you're sounding an awful lot like a vampire, but they're not real, right? Plus, you eat regular food, you can obviously be out in the daytime, and..."

A noise interrupted my rambling, and it simultaneously warmed and aroused me. He was chuckling lightly, amused by my thoughts. It was the first time I'd heard him laugh, and it immediately became my mission to hear that sound as often as possible.

"We will figure it all out, I have faith we will," Hugh said. "For now, let's discuss the plan for the next few days. When do you need to be in California?"

"I don't start work for two weeks," I told him. "I'd planned to get there a week early, to meet the movers and unpack, but that's a little flexible."

"And when are your cousins driving in to meet you?"

"I planned to meet them for dinner tomorrow."

Glancing over at him, I found his eyes were on my face. Startled, I looked away quickly. There was a gentle hum in the air, a tension between us that wasn't necessarily uncomfortable, but in the confines of the car, it was palpable.

"Are we still on track to arrive on time?" he asked, thankfully ignoring my spastic moment.

"I wanted to stop in Chicago tonight, or even push it and make it into Madison. From there, it would only be a six-hour drive into Duluth."

"How far are we from Madison?"

"About 12 hours," I responded. "If we keep our stops short, we could make it there and still get a good night's sleep."

"Madison it is, then."

Chapter 6

The small hotel boasted a pool and free, hot breakfast. As long as it had a bed and a shower, I was golden.

"Let me get us checked in," I told Hugh, pulling into the lot. "Since we don't know who's after you, the less people that see you, the better."

"Good thinking," he agreed. "I'll wait here."

Scooting into the reception area, I made sure to take a good look at each person that was in the lobby before approaching the desk. A helpful man checked me in, sliding the room key packet across the counter. Giving him a tired smile, I asked for the closest stairwell to the room from the parking lot, and he directed me to the far end of the building, where a door was accessible by room key.

Getting back into the SUV, I drove us to a parking spot next to the door and grabbed just the bag I needed. Hugh lifted the cooler easily from the back, bringing it with us to our room.

Swiping the card at the outside door, I found our room two doors down the hallway. The hotel was all on one level, spread out in a T shape. Opening our room, I flipped on all the lights before dumping my bag on a table. The room was surprisingly spacious, with two beds and a small kitchen table.

Turning to face Hugh, I found myself suddenly nervous. This morning, we'd shared an explosive kiss, and hadn't had to deal with it as we'd just spent over 12 hours in the car together where I had to focus on driving, but now I had nothing to do but look at him.

Oddly, he seemed just as uncertain, standing beside the cooler that he'd set down against the wall.

"We should get those in the fridge for tonight," I spoke, my voice unusually scratchy.

Nodding, he bent to the task, storing the leftover bags of blood in the small fridge. While he did that, I unzipped my bag, pulling out my toiletries and pajamas. Inside, I also had the clothing I'd bought for Hugh. Since we'd made it into Madison, we'd have time to stop at a store tomorrow morning to acquire more than two days' worth of outfits.

Setting his things on one of the beds, I picked up my bathroom stuff and excused myself.

"I think I'll take a shower," I told him. "Feeling kind of gross after being on the road all day."

He didn't speak, just nodded, while I escaped into the smaller room. Blasting the shower as hot as it would go, I turned to study myself in the mirror.

There were small bags under my eyes, I was sure from the stress of the last two days coupled with straining them by driving for so long. My skin was flushed, more than normal, and my hair was flat and lifeless from being in a pony tail all day. Yanking out the clip, I finger-combed through it before stepping into the hot steam.

I took my time in the shower, only delaying the inevitable. No matter how many times I washed my hair or lathered up my body wash, I would still have to face the man in the next room.

He had sparked something in me, something that was irreversible. His lips had been on my mind all day, and I wanted to gorge myself on the feast that had only been teased at this morning. My body was reacting in ways that my brain had yet to catch up to, and it was freaking me right out.

With a deep breath, I finally shut off the water and dressed quickly in my comfortable yoga pants and t-shirt. Toweling out my hair first, I brushed through it before blasting it with the hair dryer for a few minutes to help it dry. After brushing my teeth, I took the step I was fearing.

I opened the bathroom door.

Hugh was relaxing on the bed, reading through the hotel information that was left on the desk. He'd given up on the television after that morning, and I realized I could have offered him a book to peruse, at least.

He looked up and met my eye, and I stood motionless as a figure cut in stone. My heart was racing and I forgot to breathe.

Hugh rose off the bed, approaching me slowly. When he was within reaching distance, his fingers brushed my arm, wrapping loosely as they slid down to my wrist before entangling with my own fingers.

"You look exhausted," he said quietly.

Not waiting for my response, he pulled me to one of the beds, folding down the sheets and settling me between them. When I was tucked in, he turned to climb into the opposite bed.

"Hugh?" I asked tentatively. When he turned, I worked up the courage to speak my mind. "Would you stay? Beside me, I mean."

His eyes softened, his mouth quirking into a gentle smile. Without a word, he turned off the lights and slid under the covers beside me.

We faced each other in the dark, and I could feel his heat seeping into me. The steamy shower had nothing on him.

Pressing a hand gently against his chest, I felt the steady, reassuring beat of his heart. His hand reached out to brush a strand of hair from my face, twisting the long tendril between his fingers. Then, he shifted and pulled me closer, my head coming to rest against his shoulder as his arm wrapped around my back, our bodies pressed together and our legs intertwined.

Letting out a sigh of contentment, I fell easily into sleep.

I n the morning I woke in a dreamy haze, where reality and fantasy entwined. I was warm and cozy, wrapped up in a thick blanket like a human burrito, and I didn't want to wake.

A new sensation only enhanced the dreamlike state, a tingling of nerves along my neck that left my veins singing beneath my skin. The feeling moved to my lips, a soft pressure that evoked an instant response. My mouth parted on a gasp, but no air intruded. Instead, there was the gentle probing of a tongue, which I responded to in kind.

Hugh's arms tightened around me, our bodies still entangled from sleep. My nails dug into his back in an attempt to bring him closer, a need I didn't fully understand. One leg wrapped around his hip and I pressed into him, wanting to alleviate the pressure that was building inside me.

His mouth left mine and I gasped, breathless from the exchange. As his lips moved from cheek to chin, I arched back, offering him the thing he needed– the thing we both wanted.

When he made contact against my neck, I let out a soft sound of anticipation. His teeth nipped and I pressed against him, sensing the relief I was seeking to be so close I could taste it.

His tongue swept across the bite, soothing the initial sting. Then, without warning, he pulled away.

With our bodies entwined, he couldn't go far, but his lips were no longer making contact and my body screamed in protest.

"What is it? Did I do something wrong?" I asked in a small voice, terrified of the answer.

Hugh's breath was heavy, as if he were trying desperately to get under control. At my question, his hand came up to brush my cheek.

"No, of course not, it was me who almost did something wrong."

Confusion clouded my features as I thought through the last few minutes, attempting to separate dream from reality.

A cold realization swept over me at what had almost transpired.

"Oh," I said with sudden clarity. My eyes met his, and I spoke the truth. "But... I wanted it."

The hand still on my cheek shook. "Kate, please... I don't have that much control. Call me a monster, or at least look disgusted with me."

I did the last thing either of us expected. I laughed.

It did interesting things to my already electrified nerves, as my body shook against his.

"You're not a monster, Hugh," I assured him. "But, you're right. This is dangerous, at least until we know more."

"You mean like whether or not I would kill you?" he asked incredulously.

"Well... yes, for one."

Giving him a sardonic grin, I waited for him to see the humor in the situation. Though his lips didn't turn up, his body did relax slightly, and I took that as a good sign.

Deciding he needed more convincing, I closed the distance between us to press against his lips once again. This time I kept the contact light, though my body craved more. It took almost more will power than I possessed to pull away from him.

"I want this. I want *you*. Maybe not right now, but I do. It terrifies me, but not because of anything you did- it's because I've never felt this way before. My body has never responded this way to anyone, so even though we have some things to figure out," like why you want to suck my blood, and why I *want* you to, "I know, deep down, that this is right."

"You are an amazing person, Kate. If it took getting tortured to meet you, I would endure a thousand more swipes of a knife for another moment like this."

His words left me breathless. This time when our lips met, I poured all of the emotions that I was unable to express out loud into the kiss. When we finally came up for air, I made the mistake of looking at the clock.

"We should get on the road," I told him, though I made no attempt to move.

"Yes, we should," he agreed, pressing his lips to mine once more before untangling himself. "Let me take a quick shower, and we can be on our way."

Nodding my agreement, I remained where I was, too comfortable to stand up.

Right now, I should be over-analyzing everything that had just happened, and my body's responses to it, but the dreamlike haze had yet to recede, and I couldn't wipe the goofy smile from my face.

Giving myself a few more minutes, I leisurely stood and began to dress, knowing Hugh would be done shortly. After brushing my hair out, I gathered it into a loose braid over my shoulder to keep it contained.

While I packed my bag, I called my cousin, Jade. I wanted to let her know I was on track for dinner, and also that there would be an addition to our reservation.

I'd called Jade instead of Pearl, knowing I would be asked about a hundred questions less by the former.

The bathroom door opened just as I ended the call and I looked up, then stilled at the image before me. Hugh stood in the doorway with a towel wrapped low on his hips. Every muscle was on full display, water glistening against his tanned skin. A single bead dripped from his chest, racing down his abs to disappear into the towel. My eyes traced its path, my mouth suddenly dry.

He cleared his throat gently, and as my eyes snapped to his face, I realized I was gawking. The cheesy grin on his face told me he knew it, and didn't mind in the least.

"Um, clothes. You need clothes," I stammered, lifting the pile from the bed and handing it to him.

His hands trapped mine in the transfer, and his smile widened. "You're cute when you're flustered."

Narrowing my eyes, I ripped my hands from his grasp and pushed his shoulder playfully, taking him by surprise so that he was forced to take a few steps back into the bathroom.

"Get dressed, Batman," I smirked at him.

Chapter 7

Before hitting the road, Hugh and I stopped at a clothing store, and I watched in amusement as Hugh picked out and tried on several styles. I convinced him to get a couple of dressy items, just in case, along with the more casual outfits.

Happy now that he had a few things to call his own, we folded up his new purchases into a duffle and, after a coffee stop, made our way across Wisconsin.

We were about an hour from Duluth when a loud bang sounded, and my wheel jerked to the side. I gasped in alarm, realizing we'd blown a tire, and pulled over immediately.

"Son of a bitch," I grumbled.

Looking over to Hugh, who had braced against the door and looked ready to grab me and leap out of the car if need be, I gave a sigh.

"I've got a spare in the back, we'll have to clear out the bags and cooler."

After tapping on the emergency lights, we both got out to examine the damage. The rear passenger tire had blown, but the rim looked like it was in good shape, which was lucky.

Hugh and I set to work clearing out the trunk, transferring the bags into the backseat. I lifted up the cover to unveil the spare, a jack, and the other tools we'd need.

Bringing out the crow bar, I grabbed a thin piece of plastic-covered cushion, which I rolled out on the ground to kneel on. As I placed the crowbar on the first lug nut, a shadow blocked my light.

"Shouldn't you jack up the car first?"

"I always loosen first, because I'm not always strong enough in the arms and sometimes have to jump on the bar. I did that once when it was jacked up, and the whole car fell."

Hugh crouched beside me, poking at the mat with a finger.

"That is a brilliant idea," he commented.

"Yeah," I grinned, "my mom was insistent that I know the basics of a car, but that didn't mean we worked on them without style. This thing has saved my knees."

"Why don't you let me do that?" Hugh held his hand out, waiting for me to give up the crow bar.

"I can do it," I said petulantly.

"Of that I have no doubt, but you have to admit that I am just a bit more physically strong than you."

My shoulders dropped as I gauged his expression. I couldn't argue with the facts.

"You have a point. I'll grab the jack and spare."

Before I'd even set the jack at his feet, Hugh had loosened all the lug nuts. He made quick work of the jack, slipping the ruined tire off and replacing it. I watched in awe, envious of his physical abilities.

"Okay, that was the quickest tire change on record," I gawked. "You should work in a pit crew."

"That's a possible career path," he agreed lightly, lowering the vehicle again.

Then, both our shoulders sagged as the weight of the vehicle sank onto the flat spare tire.

"I don't have a pump," I announced, annoyed at the situation. "Damnit!"

I gave the tire a swift kick, then glanced down the road. A few cars had passed, though none had slowed as we obviously had this under control. Going through our options, I laid out the best plan to Hugh.

"The town we just passed had a gas station with a mechanic attached," I explained. "I'll walk to it, see if I can buy a pump or a new tire, or both."

"I'll come with you," Hugh began, but I held out my hand to stop him.

"I'd rather one of us stay with the car, in case anyone gets curious or a cop comes by. We don't want anyone seeing what we have in the cooler."

"Good point," he sighed, battling with the idea of leaving me alone.

I understood the sentiment. We hadn't been separated since we met.

"Why don't I go to the town? I can run..."

Shaking my head, I said, "You don't have ID or credit cards, and I don't have enough cash to cover it. It's best if I go, I'm sorry."

"All right, but send me updates," Hugh crossed his arms, unhappy with the situation but quickly realizing we were short on options.

"How would I do that?" I asked, my brow knitting in confusion.

"Just talk out loud," he grinned. "I'll be listening."

His casual mention of his hearing startled me, but I shook off the momentary stall.

"All right. I'll just be the crazy lady, walking down the highway talking to herself."

"That's the spirit," he winked, and I laughed appreciatively.

Grabbing my purse from the car, I started on my way. We'd passed the town just a few minutes ago, so it shouldn't take too long to reach it by foot.

I stayed on the edge of the highway, where a strip of gravel about three feet wide separated the road from grass, which led directly into towering rows of pines interspersed with oak trees. It was a beautiful part of the country, calm, with fresh air to boot.

Knowing I could easily walk a ten-minute mile, I kept my pace quick, wanting to be back to Hugh as swiftly as possible. My long legs ate up the ground, and every five minutes I would announce aloud, "I'm safe."

I had no idea if Hugh could really hear me, but had to believe he could. About half an hour later, I was at the gas station.

It was still relatively early in the afternoon, and I went straight to the mechanic's side of the building to inform them of the situation.

"We've got a tire for you," the man with grease-covered fingers told me, typing into his computer. "And a pump. You're sure there're no holes in the spare?"

"There wasn't the last time I had to use it," I told him. "Even if there is, we can drive it straight back here to replace the tire. We're only about three miles away."

He nodded, offering me an apologetic smile. "I would offer to drive you down, but I'm the only one on duty today, and I can't leave the shop. I'm real sorry about that."

"It's fine," I assured him, touched at the sentiment. "I've been driving for a couple days, I can use the exercise."

He laughed heartily at this, then rang up a pump. It was more portable, so I let him know I'd be back to get a tire put on. Or, two tires, since it was always better to replace both sides at once.

"On my way back," I spoke aloud, once I was out of earshot of the mechanic and beginning my trek.

The road seemed even more deserted, though it was a major highway. Of course, in my previous trips, I'd come to realize that most of Wisconsin wasn't exactly known for traffic.

When I judged myself to be about a mile from the car, I shifted the pump from the crook of one arm to another, and was about to announce my location when a huge, winged shadow flew overhead.

Startled by the size of whatever bird would make such an impression, I searched the sky above me, but saw nothing.

A bad feeling grew in the pit of my stomach, yet I couldn't place what gave me fear. Though I was tired, I picked up my pace again.

Two more shadows crossed my light, moving in a direct line to my car... to Hugh.

I began running now, switching to the road instead of the gravel for better purchase, my heart racing with dread. Though I didn't know what those shadows were, my gut was screaming that danger was close.

"Hugh!" I yelled out, hysterics in my voice.

My feet beat against the pavement as I put everything I had into the sprint. Something was wrong, I could feel it.

"Hugh!" I screamed again, tears stinging my eyes.

The SUV was in view now, close enough I could make out the license plate. Hugh was nowhere to be seen.

I reached the car and dropped the pump, spinning in a circle, searching for the man I realized with sudden, absolute clarity that I couldn't live without.

As I turned toward the trees, the sight nearly dropped me to my knees. Hugh was there, surrounded by three large men. He was fighting them, but he wasn't strong enough against their might. Terror seized my throat, but I forced myself forward.

"Hey!" I called out, my voice shaking but loud. "Leave him alone!"

The three men paused to take me in, and one smiled at me, a slow, wicked grin. I paused in my tracks, fighting through the heavy feeling of evil permeating the air.

"What do we have here?" the man who had smiled asked, releasing Hugh and stepping toward me. "I can't sense you. Why can't I sense you?"

He was speaking gibberish, but I bolstered my brazen attitude and called out again.

"I said, leave him alone."

The two men still gripping Hugh's arms took a step back, shaking their heads in confusion. The man who had spoken took another step toward me, seeming intrigued.

"Interesting," he breathed, and, in the blink of an eye, was suddenly in front of my face.

His hands gripped my upper arms, and I felt a chill slide through my system.

This is what evil feels like, I thought erratically.

"Who are you?" the man demanded, his hot breath washing over my face as his startling deep, almost teal blue eyes bore into mine.

My eyes were spitting fire as I struggled against the hold.

"No! Kate!" Hugh cried out, and though I couldn't seem to look away from the man in front of me, I could hear Hugh struggling.

The man squeezed my arms tighter, lifting me from the ground. I was in a daze, my surroundings blurring as we rose higher. Dimly, I realized the ground was no longer beneath my feet, nor was it beneath the man who was attacking me.

"No!" I heard Hugh's strangled cry from a distance, my gaze locked on the vile creature in front of me.

There was some kind of haze closing over my mind. My thoughts drifted, as insubstantial as the air surrounding me.

"Answer my question," the man said softly, our gazes locked.

I was unable to look away, and couldn't remember why I wanted to.

Kate! Come back to me!

Hugh's voice no longer sounded hollow, or far away. It came from inside me, and it broke the spell this evil man was weaving. With a start, reality crashed down upon me, as I realized I was 15 feet in the air.

My voice took on a new quality, echoing from somewhere deep inside, borrowing from a pool of strength I'd never tapped into before.

"*Put. Me. Down. Now!*" I yelled into the man's face.

His eyes jerked wide as we began to immediately lower, and I knew it was against his will.

Our feet touched the earth and I could read the fear now on his face.

"Let me go," I growled.

His hands released me as if they'd been burned. My attention went to the two men still struggling with Hugh, and all three watched me with wide eyes.

"Leave us now, and never return!" I commanded, and they obeyed.

All three men faded into shadows, winged creatures that lifted up and away as Hugh stared at me in shock.

Chapter 8

*H*ugh remained stock still for several more seconds, his eyes wide and jaw slacked. Then, without warning, my knees gave out and I sank to the ground.

Before I hit the hard earth, two strong arms wrapped around me, cushioning my fall.

"Kate! Kate, are you all right?" Hugh's voice sounded tinny and distant, though not as hazy as when I'd been trapped in the air with that... that man.

"What... the *hell*... just happened?" I responded, my eyes fluttering open to meet his.

They bore into me, all the fear and terror swirling in the dark depths. There was something else there, too, and I reached a hand up to brush his hair away.

"Those men, they were like me," Hugh shuddered with the realization.

Already denying the statement, I shook my head. "No, Hugh, they were pure evil. They were nothing like you."

His gaze softened at my admission, and he brought his forehead to rest against mine. I took a momentary solace in the comfort it provided.

"I heard you," I murmured, reeling from the events that just transpired. "I heard you, in my mind."

"I... I think I spoke to you, in your mind."

Pulling back so I could look him in the eye, I asked, "Did you know you had telepathy?"

"No," he answered. "At least, not that I remember."

"Try it again," I urged, curiosity winning out over the absurdity of the notion.

You terrified me, he spoke the words softly into my mind.

I reached out and pulled him to me, a soft comfort in the kiss, to assure us both that we were still here, and still alive.

As you did me, I returned, feeling completely natural to send a thought through time and space.

Hugh drew back, astonished. "Did you know *you* could do that?"

"Nope, that's a first."

He stood, pulling me to my feet along with him.

"Can you stand?"

I nodded, but held onto his upper arms just in case. Next, I inspected him for any injuries, needing to assure myself he was whole and in one piece. He did the same for me, cursing under his breath when he found fingerprint-shaped bruises along my biceps.

"I could kill him," Hugh snarled.

"Hey," I said softly, waiting for his gaze to meet mine. "I'm okay. It's just a bruise."

He took a deep breath before asking the question I knew would be coming.

"They listened to you. How did you do that?"

Biting my lip, I glanced to the SUV and the abandoned pump that lay behind it.

"Why don't we get the tires, and I'll explain once we hit the road again?"

He nodded his agreement, helping me up the bank of gravel. Leaving me to lean against the door, Hugh retrieved the pump and quickly filled the tire.

"Will you be all right to drive?"

"Yes," I told him. "Let's go."

As I walked around to the driver side door, I caught a reflection of myself in the glass. My hair had escaped from the braid, and was now shooting out at every angle. The short-sleeved shirt revealed the bruises that stood out starkly against my pale skin, so I quickly dug through one of my bags to find a cardigan to pull on over my shirt. It helped to cover the bruising, at least.

Jumping in the seat, I took out the hair tie and shook the mass loose, wavy now from the braid.

"Better?" I asked Hugh.

"You always look beautiful," he responded.

My heart gave a quick little jump. I swallowed once, then made a U-turn and headed back to the mechanic shop.

We both agreed to put the event behind us until after we were back on the road to Duluth. I was replaying everything that had happened, but I knew that neither of us truly had any answers.

The mechanic helped us immediately, which might have been partly guilt at making me walk back to the stranded car. He didn't need to know that I was grateful for that fact– how could we have explained those evil men?

It was enough that Hugh had a target on his back. We didn't need to involve any innocent bystanders.

Once we were on our way again, silence fell over us while I worked out the best way to explain why those creatures had listened to me. The best way to explain this side of myself that I'd never shared with anyone before.

"I'm not normal," I burst out, and immediately winced at my use of the phrase. "What I mean is, I discovered something about myself when I was very young, and it's something that only I can do. At least, that I know of. When it first started happening, I thought it was something everyone could do– but I quickly realized it was just me."

Hugh was silent, allowing me to tell the story in my own time. He wasn't judging me, just genuinely curious. The pressure immediately released, and I was able to continue.

"I was about 6 the first time I remember realizing something was different. I was in kindergarten, and there was this kid a couple years older who always picked on me for having red hair. He was relentless, and I was too nice to tell him to stop. There were a lot of days I went home in tears.

"Then, one day, I'd had enough. Instead of crying, I yelled back. I told him, 'leave me alone and go pick on someone your own size!' We were on the playground, and he immediately turned around and picked a fight with a boy in his grade. I found a teacher to break it up, but that little boy ended up with a broken nose, because of me."

Taking a deep breath, I looked over at Hugh.

"That bully did what I told him to do." Focusing back on the road, I continued the story, "I tried to explain it to my mom, and even though I don't think she really believed me, she gave me good advice. She told me not to tell people what to do."

At this I smiled, then tried to clarify.

"She said I should always ask people to do things for me, instead of telling them. So, if I wanted candy from a friend, I would say 'can I have some' instead of 'give me some.' I was the politest child you'd ever meet. Of course, I did slip up now and again. It was always on accident, and usually only when I was pushed hard enough."

"That must have been difficult for you to navigate as a child," Hugh murmured, his eyes on me. After a moment he added, "That's why you're able to accept me so easily."

"Partly, yes," I agreed. "But, we obviously have a greater connection."

He nodded thoughtfully. "That we do."

I slowed down as we entered the city limits of Superior, which was the city just over the bridge from Duluth. Lake Superior came into view as we drove along, the stunning blue sparkling in the late day sun.

The restaurant information was in the navigation system, and I followed its directions, driving over the Blatnik Bridge and crossing over into Minnesota.

"Look, I was thinking," I began, running my lower lip through my teeth. "We need to act as normally as possible with my cousins. I don't want them to worry."

"Tell me more about them," Hugh responded.

"Jade and Pearl are the two we're meeting with. Pearl is married to her high school sweetheart, and they have seven kids. *Seven*," I emphasized, still blown away by that fact. "Jade is a photographer; she used to live in Miami but recently moved back to Sun Valley. She's been engaged for almost a year. I met her fiancé on my last trip, his name is Talon. He was a little intimidating when I first met him, but he's the nicest guy in the world and head over heels for Jade. He'll be there, too."

"What do you mean, intimidating?"

I shrugged. It was a difficult thing to pinpoint, especially when Talon smiled and showed off his dimples. "Kind of like you, I guess. Just an understated power."

Hugh's brows wrinkled at my description. "Understated? I thought it was rather obvious."

Glancing over at him, I slapped him playfully on the arm. "You're just edging for a compliment, aren't you?"

"Yes," he answered bluntly, crossing his arms over his chest.

Rolling my eyes, I played along. "Fine. You're a big, hulking He-Man. Happy?"

"Yes. I think. What is a He-Man?"

Shaking my head, my eyes lit with humor. "Oh, I'll show you one day."

As I pulled into the lot for the restaurant, I realized just how late we were. My phone rang, and I answered it quickly.

"Hey, Jade, we're here," I began, jumping out of the car and meeting Hugh around the front to walk together. Spotting her at the entrance, I waved and said, "I see you, bye."

"Kate!" Jade exclaimed as I approached, pulling me into a hug.

She quickly released me when she noticed Hugh just behind me. Her eyes widened as she looked between him and me.

"You're... you're a..."

Whatever she was about to say was cut off as her fiancé joined us. The move was subtle, but he positioned himself between Jade and Hugh.

"Who are you?" Talon demanded of Hugh, his muscles rippling suggestively beneath his skin.

Intimidating, I sent to Hugh, using our newfound path.

Jade's head perked up, staring at me in a way that made me somewhat uncomfortable. Needing to diffuse the odd situation, I stepped beside Hugh and linked my hand with his, showing solidarity.

"Jade, Talon, this is Hugh."

These people seem frightened of me, Hugh responded, with a combination of amusement and confusion.

"Nice to meet you," Jade piped up, still standing behind Talon.

She rested her hand against Talon's upper arm, and it seemed to relax him.

"Jade," I said slowly, "You were about to say something before Talon came out. What was it?"

Jade seemed hesitant, but this was important. I hated using something I'd always been so careful with, but we didn't have time to mess around.

"Tell me what you were going to say, Jade."

Hugh stiffened beside me, realizing I was using my power. Jade turned to look at Hugh directly.

"You're an Elemental."

Chapter 9

There was silence as Hugh and I both registered what Jade had just said.

What in the world was an Elemental? And why did Jade know?

The door opened and another man emerged, an aura of danger arriving with him. His deep, glittering green eyes were set in a glare and locked in on Hugh, while the tattoos covering the majority of his arms seemed to leap to life. They were mesmerizing, and I found myself taking an automatic step back.

Hugh braced me with his arm, and his touch broke the momentary haze. Shaking my head, I looked to my cousin to explain.

"Dominic, this is my cousin, Kate," Jade spoke up, realizing how explosive the situation was. "And this is her friend, Hugh."

"You bring an unknown Elemental here?" Dominic growled the accusation, though I wasn't sure if it was directed at me or Jade.

Either way, I wasn't impressed, and was feeling an inordinate amount of pressure.

"Okay, everybody back off!" I announced, throwing my hands out. All three took an involuntary step back, and I found that fact disproportionately pleasing. "This is Hugh and he's a good man. He has memory loss, and we're trying to figure out what's going on. You two and your threatening postures aren't helping."

Narrowing my own eyes at the two men, I waited to make sure my point came across.

"Now, Jade, please tell me what an Elemental is."

She suppressed a smirk at my temper, but obliged me. "There's a lot to it, but the basics are this: an Elemental is a species that has control over the elements. They are fast, strong, and also able to shift into other forms."

Her explanation left me breathless, and I shot Hugh a sidelong look.

Shift? Into other forms?

If I have this ability, I am unaware of it.

"And you're talking telepathically right now, which is why I know Hugh isn't a shadowman."

She directed the last declaration to Dominic, and he nodded thoughtfully. This made no sense to me, but it was just one in a long line of questions.

"Shadowman?" I asked aloud, but the thought echoed in my mind.

You think that's the creatures we came across on our way here. Hugh made it a statement, not a question.

"It seems we have a lot to discuss, but we have two people inside waiting for us to join them for dinner," Talon was the voice of reason. "Kate, Hugh, we invited Dominic and Reese here tonight. Reese is new to this information, and Pearl doesn't know anything about it. Will you be able to carry on a normal conversation around them?"

It took me a moment to reel in my wayward thoughts. Looking at Jade, I was suddenly seeing her in a new light.

"You're one too, aren't you?" I breathed the question, almost afraid of the answer.

"Yes," she affirmed, then wrapped an arm around my shoulder. "And we can have a long talk once this dinner is over, and we get Pearl safely to the hotel."

Taking a deep breath, I nodded over to Talon, easing his mind that we would do our best to act normally. Squeezing the hand still wrapped around mine, I allowed Jade to lead us inside.

Sitting with Pearl was a pretty woman with long brunette hair and eyes the color of milk chocolate. Her gaze met mine and I felt an odd sort of kinship with her, though we'd never met before.

After being introduced, I sat beside Hugh, who had chosen a spot next to Pearl. The view of the lake out the window- including the lift bridge Duluth was famous for- was breathtaking, but I couldn't focus on it. I talked with Pearl, though that was easy- once you got her started, you only had to nod and smile to keep her going.

All the revelations from outside swirled around my mind, and I was close to hyperventilating. The only solid reassurance was Hugh at my side, as he casually took my hand and gave me a gentle squeeze now and again to remind me that I wasn't alone.

That small gesture reassured me, grounded me, and even though his gaze constantly swept the restaurant making it seem he wasn't paying attention, I knew that wasn't true.

I smiled brightly at Pearl as she showed me the newest pictures of her twins, who were about to be 6 months old.

"I can't believe you're able to be away from them," I said.

"I do miss them like crazy, all the kids, but it's good for Micah to try his hand at wrangling them all."

"So, your mom is helping?" I asked with a grin.

"Oh, without a doubt," she winked at me. "That is, if she's not busy planning the wedding."

Glancing over at Jade, I asked the obvious, "For Jade?"

Pearl rolled her eyes. "No. Those two are being stubborn and decided on a long engagement. They're already living together, I mean, what's the point?"

Chuckling at her small rant, I then asked, "So, whose wedding is it?"

"Emma! Rick popped the question last week!"

Emma was the second oldest of the family. She'd gone through a difficult divorce about a year ago, and I was glad to hear she was happy.

"That was fast," I commented.

"They're so right for each other," Pearl shrugged this off. "When it's right, why wait?"

Her voice rose in volume on the last part, and her gaze landed on Jade. We both looked to the other woman, who had crammed an entire overstuffed ravioli into her mouth.

"What?" she asked, though it came out muffled.

Pearl rolled her eyes again. "See what I'm working with here?"

Reese was staring at Jade in awe, and Talon noticed.

With a conspiratorial grin, he told her, "She's always like this."

Jade paused with the fork halfway to her mouth, still chewing her previous bite.

"What?" she said again, her cheeks puffed out like a chipmunk.

We all laughed. Hugh even twitched a smile, and spoke into my mind.

I like your family.

The short observation left a warm feeling in my chest.

Me, too.

Swallowing what was in her mouth, Jade spoke again. "I'm from Wisconsin. I like to eat."

"Yeah, so am I, and I've never eaten like you," Pearl retorted.

Shrugging, Jade ripped off another chunk of bread. "I've got a good metabolism."

Being an Elemental probably had something to do with that.

As the conversation dwindled, we made our way out the door. Talon and Dominic exchanged a few words before Dominic steered Reese away from the restaurant, and onto the walking path lining the lake. I watched them for a moment before turning to my cousins.

"I'm pretty wiped," I told them.

"Why don't we all head to the hotel?" Jade suggested.

It was a ruse to get Pearl to safety, and it seemed to work.

"If you're all going to bed, I'll call Gabi and have her come hang out," Pearl announced.

"Great, we're getting kicked out of the hotel," Jade groaned.

"Ha! I'm an old married woman," Pearl denied.

Jade nudged her sister playfully. "And that makes a difference how?"

Enjoying their bickering, I unlocked my doors and slid into the driver seat.

Hugh and I followed Talon, Jade and Pearl to the hotel that was just a mile from the restaurant.

Saying goodnight to Pearl, Hugh and I made our way down the third-floor hall and to our room. We were still in the downtown area, and I was impressed by the view of our room once we'd checked in. The lift bridge was up, and a large ship was passing through to the bay, where it would get loaded with coal, iron ore pellets, or some other resource.

Hugh approached me while I watched, his arms wrapping around my waist. I leaned back into him, letting out a sigh of contentment.

Though Jade had opened a whole new slew of questions, it was a relief to be around someone- make that *three* someone's- who would be able to help Hugh.

"Elemental," I said quietly as the ship blared its horn. "Does that sound familiar at all?"

"No," Hugh responded. "But, at least we're on the right track. What are the odds you're related to someone like me?"

Shaking my head, I answered, "That's the thing. She wasn't always an Elemental. Is it something a person can become?"

"We will find out," Hugh promised, dropping a kiss onto my temple. "Are you ready?"

Shrugging, I glanced down at myself. I was still wearing the same clothes as I'd worn all day driving, with the addition of the sweater to hide the bruising on my upper arms. The excuse to get Pearl back to the hotel hadn't been a lie– I *was* wiped, but the promise of answered questions gave me the strength I needed.

There was a knock on the door, and I stepped away from Hugh's warmth to answer it. Suddenly I realized that Hugh had heard them coming, which had prompted him to ask if I was ready. Things like that would certainly take a lot of getting used to.

Jade and Talon stood on the other side of the door. Jade took one look at my exhausted expression and wrapped me in a hug.

"I know this is a lot to take in, but I'm here for you," she whispered.

Nodding, I stepped back to allow them into the room. There were two leather chairs, which Talon arranged closer to the edge of one of the beds. Jade plopped into one, while Talon sat in the other. I made myself comfortable on the end of the bed, gesturing for Hugh to join me.

Crossing my legs under me, I leaned into Hugh when he wrapped his arm around my back.

"Where should we start?" Jade asked in general.

Talon spoke up. "Hugh, tell us what you remember."

"I escaped from... somewhere. It was some kind of facility outside of Boston. I remember running, and needing a place to hide.

There were men chasing me. I came upon a parking lot, and thought to hide in a vehicle. Luckily, I chose Kate's."

"When I discovered him in my trunk, he was near death," I added, skipping over the heart attack I'd almost had when Hugh had sneezed. "I had to help him. We stopped at a motel and cleaned his wounds. There were... there were crisscrossed marks all over his chest, and one particularly deep wound that I stitched up. Hugh was unconscious for all of that."

Jade looked impressed, while Talon's expression was one of concern. "You remember nothing before that?"

Hugh shook his head.

"There's more," I continued. "When we were about an hour away, we had a tire blow."

Reliving the terrifying moments with the men who turned to shadows, I stopped as Talon suddenly stood, his fist clenched, pacing away from us.

"Shadowmen," he growled, turning back.

"You said that earlier," I remembered. "You said you knew Hugh wasn't one. What is a shadowman?"

Jade sighed, fielding the question. "From what we understand, a shadowman is an Elemental who has given into the darkness."

"They give up their souls for power, and become wholly evil," Talon added, his fists still clenched.

"And how did you know Hugh wasn't one of these shadowmen?" I asked.

Jade shifted uncomfortably. "The fact that you are able to speak telepathically– well, that's something only two types of relationships can do."

Blinking once, I glanced over at Hugh. He looked back at me with the same expression I was sure was on my own face.

"What are they? The types of relationships?" I asked, without looking away.

Jade hesitated before answering, clearly not wanting to be the one to reveal this information.

Finally, with sigh, she said, "Twins, and... mates."

Chapter 10

Sucking in a breath, I turned away from Hugh to stare at Jade. Somewhere in the recesses of my brain, I was flipping through every moment of my time with Hugh. From my illogical decision to help a wounded man, to accepting his need for blood and even helping him break into a hospital to get some, and certainly not least, my physical reaction to his presence.

While I was floored by the revelation, a large part of me felt relief at having my unusual behavior explained.

"And we're definitely not twins," I finally murmured.

Kate...

I shook my head, but answered in my mind. *Not now. We'll talk about that once we're alone.*

His arm tightened around my waist, but he said nothing more.

"Okay, let's get back on track," I said, pushing away the mix of emotions that had surfaced. "What do the shadowmen want? Why were they after Hugh?"

Jade and Talon exchanged a look before Jade answered. "That's the strange part. They've always been after the women."

"To get their souls back," I pieced together. My brow furrowed, thinking through our encounter. "The shadowmen were definitely surprised to see me, which meant they weren't using Hugh to get to me."

"How were you able to defeat three of them?" Jade asked, leaning forward.

Shifting uncomfortably, I took a deep breath before spilling my secret. It was a difficult thing to do, as I'd been hiding this particular quirk since it had manifested itself more than 20 years ago, but these were not exactly normal times.

"I'm able to control the actions of others by telling them what to do," I told them, before delving into a deeper explanation.

While I described my ability to them, Jade's eyes grew wide.

"That's incredible," she sat back, clearly thinking through the ramifications of my revelations.

"Kate, I believe you're a type of shield," Talon ventured. "Which explains why, when we first met, I wasn't able to peg you as one of the Gifted."

"Back up. Shield? Gifted?"

Talon smiled apologetically. "The Gifted are humans that have latent abilities. They are also able to be converted into Elementals. It seems your power is very strong, as it manifested at such a young age, and as a human."

"What, exactly, is a shield?" I asked, intrigued by the notion.

"You're able to influence those around you. Like, right now, you're hiding the fact that you're Gifted. I believe that is what has kept you safe. I believe those shadowmen were hunting Hugh, and were only able to sense him once you were apart- when you left to walk to the mechanic."

Hugh and I both absorbed this information, though it made little sense to me.

"So, you're saying that I'm naturally bouncing your own thoughts back to you, to keep my identity a secret? That I can influence your thoughts or your actions?"

"Yes," Talon answered, "that is a good way to describe it."

I leaned back. "Huh. Gives a whole new meaning to 'I'm rubber you're glue,' doesn't it?"

After a few chuckles, Jade spoke up. "Hugh, I believe I can help you unlock your memories."

"How?" I asked, sitting straight again.

"I'm an empath, and I'm able to connect to other people's emotions, their memories. It's still new for me, but I would like to try."

It's your call, I sent to Hugh.

He nodded. "I'll do whatever is necessary."

"Dominic offered his home to us," Talon interjected. "It is secluded and protected."

"Let's go, then," I offered, standing and dragging Hugh up with me.

We drove together in silence, up the hill to the northeast. Houses became more interspersed, and the natural wooded area became more prevalent. Talon drove down several dirt roads, eventually finding a trail only recognizable by the tire tracks that had come before us.

Talon slowed to drive through the trees, barely scraping by along each side. Just as I was doubting whether there was actually a residency in these woods, the space opened to reveal a small structure.

The outside was made from logs, and blended easily into its surroundings. The trees were so thick, their branches reached across the roof, easily enclosing the cozy cabin.

We parked behind the only other car, and I spotted two figures on the steps. Jade bounced right over to them, while Hugh was more conservative. I paused with him, assessing the situation.

"Thanks for inviting us out here," Jade grinned at Dominic and Reese, clearly at ease. "You have a beautiful property."

"Thank you," Dominic responded, seemingly pleasant.

He led the way into the main room, which was sparsely decorated and fit his personality to a T.

Jade ignored the leather couch and plopped down on the floor, Talon scooting in behind her to give her back a place to rest. Hugh sat opposite Jade, and I chose the leather couch, close enough to Hugh to place a reassuring hand on his shoulder.

"I will watch over you all," Dominic assured us, and I attempted to calm my nerves.

Dominic and Reese retreated to the kitchen island, while Talon spoke to the room.

"When we did this with our friend Lani, it took several hours, though it didn't seem that long to either Jade or Lani."

Hugh turned to search my gaze, emotion swirling in his eyes. He was nervous, I realized, and I smiled gently at him.

It will be all right. I'm here, watching over you.

With a slight nod of his head, Hugh turned back to Jade. She closed her eyes in concentration, and Hugh followed suit. I didn't move, lending my strength through the palm of my hand. There was utter silence as the minutes ticked by, turning into an hour or more. Though my body began to ache, I refused to move, worry becoming a living, breathing thing the more time that passed.

Suddenly, without warning, Jade's eyes shot open, followed by Talon's and Hugh's. They blinked at each other, bringing reality back after the foray into Hugh's mind.

"What happened?" I finally burst out, unable to contain my curiosity any longer.

"We've uncovered one fact," Hugh's shoulders sagged in relief. "Everything else was just... a blur."

Jade nodded, "Blurry, but not black. I think, with time, your memories will return to you. For now, at least you have the one thing to go on."

"What is it?" I asked, my eyes on the man before me.

He watched me a long time before answering. "I know what I was doing before I was caught."

There was complete silence once again, until I found my voice. "What were you doing?"

Hugh looked over to Talon, an understanding passing between them. Then, he switched his gaze to Dominic as he answered.

"There is a group that is hunting our kind. They don't differentiate between the shadowmen and Elementals. They capture and torture whomever they believe to be supernatural. The majority of their captives are innocents."

The anger in Hugh's voice had me sinking to the floor, wrapping one arm around his waist and placing the other on his chest.

I'm here.

It was as if a wave of fresh air cleared his tense features. Calmer now, Hugh continued.

"I'm not sure how I found out about these camps, but I remember working to shut them down. They've developed a serum that can incapacitate our kind. That's what I was shot with, and what has caused me to lose my memories. I managed to escape, but with no memory, I didn't even know where to run."

"We are heading out to the southwest anyway, so we will come with you to California. It will give you extra protection, and we can work on your memories more," Jade said, and I looked to her in surprise.

"Lani is working to find others of our kind," Talon said before I could speak. "Perhaps we can uncover who is behind these torture camps. It would also be nice to find a healer."

"What's a healer?" Reese asked, her interest piqued.

"Many of our people have abilities that go beyond element manipulation. Healers are similar to doctors, but more. From what my mother told me, they are able to connect their spirit to the person who is ill, and heal them from the inside out," Talon explained.

"That sounds incredible," Reese breathed.

Talon asked Dominic about his tattoos, which I had also been curious about.

Though he seemed uncomfortable being the center of attention, Dominic answered the question.

"My tattoos are symbols from Elemental spells. From what my parents explained to me as a child, Elementals have origins in every culture. Native Americans," he gestured toward Talon, then toward Jade and I when he continued, "Irish, wherever Hugh's from. Every part of the world has a trace of magic, if you look closely enough. At one time, Elementals were more connected, and had their own language that superseded each region. My parents taught the language to my brother and me when we were young."

We all contemplated what Dominic told us, and Jade was the first to speak up.

"We need to rebuild. No one should spend so many years alone." Here, she squeezed Talon's hand, and I wondered briefly what she meant. "It seems Elementals could be such a force for good. We need to find as many as we can, figure out a way to reconnect."

Talon immediately backed Jade's words. "It is easier said than done, but I agree wholly."

"As do I," Dominic added, surprising us all. "I have a twin brother, who is hunting a shadowman in Europe. Before we became hunters, we were inseparable, and happy. Our parents taught us much of the old ways, while also ignoring their own gifts. It was their downfall. We can prevent that from happening to others. Allow our children to grow in a safe, happy environment."

Reese seemed flabbergasted by his speech, and even though I'd just met the stoic man, I knew this was out of character for him.

"You can turn into a wolf," Reese whispered, her voice hoarse. "You, and your brother. Gray and red-brown wolves."

It was Dominic's turn to be dumbfounded. "How do you know that?"

"I... I dreamt it," Reese answered.

More silence. My brain was filled to the capacity with revelations, and I was glad Jade had something to say.

"You connected with his memories. I did the same with Talon."

Reese's wide-eyed gaze switched to Jade and back to Dominic. It was clear to me that Reese and Dominic were, as Jade had put it, mates, but it didn't seem to have registered with Reese yet.

We said our goodbyes shortly after, as it was evident Reese and Dominic had some things they needed to discuss.

∞ ∞ ∞

*W*hen we reached the hotel, all I could think about was climbing into bed and knocking out for the next eight hours.

"I feel bad about leaving Pearl all alone," I said to Jade.

"Oh, I'm sure she had a great time with Gabi," Jade reassured me. "They grew up together, and Gabi lives here now so I'm sure they found some kind of trouble to get into."

That made me feel better. My eyes blinked, heavy with sleep, and Jade took pity on me.

"We'll see you in the morning," Jade told me. "No rush."

Nodding, I allowed Hugh to guide me to our room. When we were alone, I was too tired to feel awkward.

"I know we have a lot to discuss," I told him, "and I definitely want to have that conversation, but..."

"You need to rest first," Hugh finished.

He approached me, cupping my cheek and looking deep into my eyes.

"Your well-being will always come first."

That curious, slow melting that had been happening in his presence continued at his words. Quickly changing into pajamas, I crawled into bed, Hugh following my lead.

Once I turned on my side, Hugh's body curved naturally around mine while his arm slung across my middle.

As soon as I closed my eyes, I was down for the count.

Chapter 11

Sliding my eyes open, I was momentarily blinded by a bright light seeping through the curtains. Though I was still groggy, my brain was fully functioning and the entire night's conversation flooded my thoughts.

Turning to my back, I reached out and realized Hugh was gone. I sat up with a gasp, seizing with anxiety.

The door opened and Hugh appeared, toting two coffee cups.

"Good morning," he smiled, approaching the bed and offering one of the beverages.

I accepted it, my racing heart slowing to its normal rhythm.

"Good morning," I answered, taking a sip of the sweet beverage. It was exactly how I liked it. "How long have you been up?"

"Not too long," he answered, sinking onto the bed beside me. "You needed the rest, so I thought I'd surprise you with your caffeine fix."

"Much appreciated," I smiled, taking another sip. Working up the courage to meet his eye, I said simply, "So."

"So," he mimicked, nodding sagely. "About what Jade said."

Letting out a breath, I attempted to form the words to explain how I felt.

"It's pretty obvious there's something between us," I began. "I won't deny that. Even though we've known each other for such a short time, I have a hard time being away from you. Like yesterday, when I walked to the mechanic on my own, every step I took felt like I was leaving a piece of myself behind. My body wants yours— that was pretty apparent yesterday morning. And... my blood... it comes alive near you. Like its screaming at me to give into the feeling... to become wholly yours."

Pressing my lips together, I stared at the cup in my hands as I played with the lid. Hugh was silent, knowing I had more to say, and I appreciated the moment to gather the last of my courage.

"While I can't deny any of that, I also believe in free will. This notion of mates, like neither of us has a choice in the matter, it doesn't sit well with me, but I'm also not denying it could be a possibility. I just... I'd like to take things at our own pace."

Hugh placed a fingertip under my chin, raising it delicately until my eyes met his.

"You are everything to me," Hugh said plainly. "And I want to give you everything I am, but that's not possible until I know *who* I am. Taking our time, figuring out this connection between us at our own pace— I completely agree."

With infinite tenderness, Hugh lowered his head until our lips met. The touch was so soft and gentle, I was surprised by the smoldering fire it created.

On second thought, perhaps we should dive in and fan these flames...

Hugh pulled away, a glimmer of humor in his eyes.

"What?" I asked, eyes wide.

"Your thought was very loud."

Color matching my hair seeped into my cheeks. "Oops."

"Why don't you get dressed? We are meeting with your father today, are we not?"

With a groan, I climbed out of the bed, taking a long pull on the hot drink.

"Yes, we are," I told him. "How do you feel about being introduced... as my boyfriend?"

Hugh considered this, a teasing smirk on his face. "I suppose that is better than 'potential mate,' is it not?"

Rolling my eyes, I grabbed my bag and headed into the bathroom.

∞　∞　∞

My dad lived in the smaller suburb northwest of downtown Duluth. The land was flat, the houses were further apart and there was no breathtaking view of the lake.

The temperature also rose about 20 degrees, which was still the strangest phenomenon to me. Most of the summer, downtown

Duluth and Superior suffered the effects of the enormous lake- aptly called the lake effect. Because of its size, Lake Superior basically created its own weather patterns. That meant cooler temperatures near the lake, while going up the hill onto flat land, though mere minutes away, awarded us with actual summer temperatures.

Of course, on the flip side, my dad experienced harsher winters than his close neighbors. He told me once that in a single day, he would easily get a foot of snow while the lower elevation would barely get a dusting. That wasn't always true, though- it all depended on the lake's mood.

Personally, I thought anyone living here year-round was nuts. Give me a tropical island any day.

I was slightly nervous, introducing Hugh to my father. Even though I hardly knew him myself, I realized his opinion on my choice of... boyfriend... mattered.

"Is your father married?" Hugh asked as I turned off the main road.

"No," I answered him. "He was, but he's divorced. Last time we spoke, he'd just started dating someone new, but I don't think I'll be meeting her."

"If he asks about my life, my family- what should I tell him?" Hugh asked next.

I sighed, realizing that could be tricky.

"I'll do my best to steer him away from that subject, but in case you have to give any detail, let him know you're from out of the country," I cleared my throat here, remembering something from the first night we met. "When you were in and out of consciousness the first night we met, you said something to me that I nearly forgot until now. You told me my hair was the same color as a kakabeak flower."

Hugh stilled, his expression frozen in place.

"Kakabeak..." he murmured, and I frowned over at him.

"Are you remembering something?" I asked, excitement lining my tone.

He shook his head– not in denial, but as if trying to clear it.

"I'm not sure. Just a flash of an image, really. A large house... and a garden," he added before giving up in frustration. "I know what a kakabeak is, though. I was correct in comparing your hair to its beauty."

My lips quirked into a half smile.

"Thank you," I responded. "I was curious about it, so I did an internet search after you fell back asleep. The kakabeak flower is indigenous to New Zealand. There's a good chance that's where you're from."

His gaze turned thoughtful, though there was no revelation with this information.

"All right, we can tell your father I'm from New Zealand. It's as good a place to start searching as any, also. What shall we say I do for a living?"

"Consulting, like me," I told him. "No one really knows what a consultant is, anyway."

Pulling the car to a stop, I turned to Hugh. He was dressed for the day in jeans and a snug t-shirt, and it took me a moment to speak.

"You're sure about this?"

"Yes," he answered, moving quickly to get out of the car and open my own door. "After you, girlfriend."

Holding back laughter, I led the way to the front door, taking deep breaths to steady myself. My dad answered quickly, as if he'd been watching out the window.

"Kate!" he exclaimed, wrapping me in a bear hug.

When he pulled back to examine me, his green eyes– the same color as mine– missed nothing. They zoomed in on Hugh almost immediately.

"You must be the man I've heard nothing about," he observed, his arms crossed and his eyes narrowed.

My dad's Irish heritage was prevalent in his coloring; his skin pale and freckled, his ginger hair streaked with gray. I took after him in the most obvious ways, while the shape of my eyes and the curve of my nose came from my mother.

Before I could ease over the moment, Hugh stuck his hand out.

"Yes sir, I'm Hugh. You've heard nothing because there's not much to tell, I'm afraid."

After a moment's pause, my dad burst into loud laughter, shaking Hugh's proffered hand and slapping him on the back.

"Call me Harris. Come in, come in! I want to hear everything about this new job."

With a wink in Hugh's direction, I stepped into the house and slipped off my shoes, following my dad toward the kitchen. There was a small dining room attached, and I gestured for Hugh to take a seat at the table.

"Can I get you kids something to drink? Water, tea, coffee?"

"Coffee would be great," I responded, to which my dad rolled his eyes.

"How did I know? Hugh, what can I get you?"

"Coffee sounds perfect," Hugh answered.

While my dad pulled mugs down and poured the waiting liquid, I squeezed Hugh's hand under the table.

So far, so good, I sent to him.

If we can just keep the conversation to how amazing you are, this shouldn't be a problem, he sent back.

I felt as if I was sinking into his dark gaze, and for the time I forgot where we were, and that we were not alone.

My dad cleared his throat, clearly uncomfortable at having interrupted a private moment. I jumped, then accepted the mug from him with a sheepish grin.

"Thanks, Dad," I said.

It had taken me awhile to call him Dad instead of Harris, but it now felt like the most natural thing in the world.

"Thank you, Harris," Hugh said, also accepting his drink.

My dad settled in a chair across from us.

"What time are your cousins joining us?" he asked.

"11:00," I told him. "Or maybe earlier, as I understand Talon will be cooking brunch?"

"Say what you want about him, but the boy can cook," my dad grinned, seeming excited at the prospect of a home cooked meal. He wasn't much for culinary adventures.

"I only met Talon last night, but I have a difficult time imagining him in a little apron," Hugh pointed out. "Will it have frilly lace along the edge?"

My dad and I both laughed at the image.

"Gosh, I hope not," I told him fervently.

"What about you, Hugh? Do you enjoy cooking?" my dad asked.

Hugh answered so smoothly, I wouldn't have known there was hesitation on his end if I hadn't been watching for it.

"I haven't had much time to learn, but I'm always game for adding to my list of skills."

"Women like a man who can cook," my dad told him, as if I wasn't sitting right there. "Where are you from? I can't place your accent."

"New Zealand," Hugh answered. "Though I've been in Boston on business."

"Hugh runs a consulting business," I provided.

"Really? What does that entail?"

"Uh, well, people pay me to tell them what to do," Hugh answered.

It earned another laugh from my dad.

Good answer, I told him.

"Hugh's also in marketing," I explained to my dad. "That's how we met."

"Speaking of, I want to hear all about the new job," my dad said.

After that, I managed to keep the topic on me, and my new job. Jade, Talon and Pearl arrived around 10:30, bags of food in their arms.

"How many people are you planning on feeding?" my dad asked, taking in the sheer amount of groceries.

"You've seen Jade eat, haven't you?" Pearl grinned at her uncle before settling at the table beside me.

Jade shrugged at the dig. "She has a point."

Talon unloaded the items on the counters, seeming right at home in my father's kitchen. Hugh stood and offered a hand.

"How are you with a knife?" Talon asked, his brow raised.

"Guess we'll find out," he answered.

As the men began preparing the meal, Jade slid into the chair Hugh had vacated.

Pearl looked tired, evidence of her late night in her droopy expression.

"Sorry to ditch out on you," I told her. "Did you have fun with Gabi?"

"Oh, a blast. She brought a bottle of wine to the room, and we binged on chocolate and romantic comedies."

"That sounds fun," I grinned at her over the rim of my mug of coffee.

Her eyes trailed back to the men in the kitchen, amusement dancing across her face.

"Hot, *and* he knows how to cook?" Pearl observed. "You hit the jackpot, girl."

Chuckling, I told her, "The jury's still out on his culinary skills."

"Still, though," Pearl's tone turned serious. "You look happy."

Not knowing how to respond, I nodded at her before glancing over to the subject of our conversation. Talon was demonstrating how to flip an omelet, and Hugh was studying the technique with a serious gaze. Once the eggs were safely turned, his eyes met mine, and even with everything so topsy-turvy, I felt myself settle.

There was a sudden certainty that as long as I had Hugh beside me, everything would be just fine.

Chapter 12

$\mathcal{W}$e left my dad's in the late afternoon, and while Jade, Talon and Pearl decided to do some shopping downtown, Hugh and I took a different route. Just over the lift bridge was a place known as Park Point— while the long strip of land was still part of the city, it was technically an island and its own community.

Hugh and I drove in silence, though it was comfortable. Continuing down the main street, past smaller houses stuffed together in order to claim beachfront property, past cozy bed and breakfasts, and into the short stretch of million-dollar homes, we finally came to the end of the road. There was a small airport, offering tours on propeller planes, and beyond that, there was a walking path.

"Up for a walk?" I asked Hugh, brow raised in challenge.

"With you? Always."

Enjoying the little flip of my heart his words gave, I got out of the car, grabbing my sunglasses on the way, and faced the small knoll of sand directly across from us.

"Just over that hill is the beach," I told Hugh, pointing. "But, there's a fun hike past the airport."

"I'm game," he grinned, taking my hand.

We walked together through a gate and onto a dirt path. This led us along the fence of the airport, with the higher ground to our left effectively blocking our view of the water. As we approached the copse of trees, I took the lead, following the trail directly into the thick wood.

The trail was well used, in some places wide enough for two to walk comfortably, while other times forcing us single file. With the trees rising above, it was difficult to tell the largest body of freshwater was just a few hundred feet from where we walked.

"What are your thoughts about everything?" I asked as we came to a break in the trees, passing a water station before picking the trail up on the other side.

"I am trying not to be frustrated by my memory loss. Everything that has been revealed is a lot to take in."

"Tell me about it," I murmured, glancing sidelong at my hiking companion.

Physically, at least, Hugh seemed to be in top shape. He hadn't even broken a sweat, even though we were keeping up a good pace, and his breath was even.

Maybe that was an Elemental thing.

"Being able to shift into another form is appealing to me," Hugh continued after a moment. "Though I have no idea how to even attempt such a thing."

"Maybe Talon could walk you through it," I suggested.

"That is a good idea," he agreed easily.

"I had a thought about the shadowmen who attacked us," I said. "They were coming after you, obviously, but you said the camps you were shutting down were run by humans. Do you think the shadowmen and humans are teaming up? Or maybe that the humans are being controlled and don't know it?"

"From what I remember, I had no knowledge of shadowmen being involved, but it makes sense. As to why they're behind it– I have no idea."

We both pondered the question as we continued down the path, occasionally catching snippets of the smaller bay to our right, while the larger portion of the lake still remained hidden from view. An abandoned building sat off the trail, and I looked at it with a raised brow.

"That's random."

"You've never walked this far?" Hugh asked.

"No, I've only been here with my dad, so we usually walk over the hill to the beach at the pump station. There's a lighthouse at the end of this strip that I've always wanted to walk to, but didn't want to push him."

"I'm glad I get to see it with you," Hugh said, lifting our connected hands to kiss the back of mine.

Our eyes met and the flutters in my stomach increased. Instead of baffling over the intensity of my reaction to the man I'd only known a few days, I enjoyed the sensation.

We'd stopped moving, our gazes locked. The tension built up around us, a gentle hum cushioning us in our own little bubble.

Hugh's palm cupped my neck, his opposite hand sliding around my waist. My hands came to rest against his chest, the steady beat of his heart settling my own.

As his head dropped, our eyes slid closed, and our lips met in a soft embrace.

The air surrounding us thickened, glowing with a pale-yellow light. I was dimly aware of this as the light hit my lids, but as our kiss deepened, a memory slammed into me. In an instant all remnants of reality wiped away, and I was thrown into a whole other world.

Standing in a copse of trees not unlike the ones along the hiking trail, filtered sunlight danced across my skin. Closing my eyes in concentration, I began murmuring words that were at once gibberish and perfectly clear.

The air began to shimmer with power. Throwing my head back, I opened my eyes to watch as the barrier turned invisible.

We would be protected here, if only for a little while.

Turning, I used my speed to arrive at a huge, white house. There was a garden to the side, but I had no time today to enjoy it.

A woman tore out of the house, her tear-streaked face stopping my heart.

Mother.

"They're here," she cried out. "You need to run. Get your brother to safety."

Hugh and I broke apart with a gasp, our gazes locked and searching. The soft yellow light dissipated as we stared, and as it faded completely, I spoke.

"What *was* that?"

"I... I don't know. I think it was a memory," Hugh answered, visibly shaken.

"You saw it too, right?" I wanted to verify.

"Yes," he confirmed. "Kate... I think you're helping me remember."

For a moment I was silent, my thoughts running a mile a minute. Something Jade had said the night before suddenly made sense.

"Last night, Jade told Reese that she had connected to Dominic's memories. Jade and Reese both had dreams of Talon and Dominic's lives. Do you think that's what's happening here?"

"I wish I could tell you yes or no," Hugh said, visibly frustrated with his perceived shortcomings.

"Hey," I said softly, reaching out to grip his hand again. "We're in this together, remember?"

He nodded, but was staring at the ground, refusing to meet my eye. Stepping close again, I lifted my free hand to his face, resting my palm against his cheek.

"The first time we kissed, when you remembered your name, was it anything like that?"

My question caused him to look at me curiously.

"Not exactly. It wasn't a full memory, just information restored."

So, if our first kiss gave him his name, and this more intense moment gave him a memory, what would happen if– or, more likely, when– we got intimate?

Keeping those thoughts to myself, I said the only comforting thing that came to mind.

"Your mother was beautiful. And she spoke of your brother– perhaps you do have family out there, after all."

Letting out a breath, Hugh nodded.

My lips tipped up in a smile, wanting to distract him from the gloomy look on his face.

"Still want to see the lighthouse?"

He smiled back, though it didn't fully reach his eyes. "I do."

The trail wound its way toward the water, until we were walking on sand instead of solid ground. As the bulk of the lake came into view, I paused to take it in.

"I can see why people live here," I said aloud. "Though, I don't know that I'd survive a winter."

"It is beautiful," Hugh agreed.

He moved then, to the water's edge. I followed slowly, curious about what he was going to do. When he was within a couple of feet of the calm waves, he squatted, placing his palms against the sand.

For several moments he remained there, gazing at the water. Before my incredulous eyes, the waves grew, reaching out to meet his fingertips. The rest of the lake remained calm, but in this one spot, the water responded to his touch.

Hugh lifted his hands, the water moving with him, forming into shapes. With a swift intake of breath, I stumbled forward, wanting to be closer but still keeping a healthy distance.

The water swirled, rising above Hugh's palms in an intricate dance. It morphed from fluid movement to the shape of a face, long hair flowing in the wind, droplets spiraling out before rejoining the lake.

It was my face, though not how I saw myself. This woman was strong, proud, and beautiful. The lips tipped up into a smile before Hugh released his hold, and the water went crashing back to earth.

He turned and stood, a little boy's grin on his face. My jaw was hanging open in awe, words escaping me.

Registering the look on my face, Hugh stepped forward, though he didn't make contact.

"Are you all right?"

"That was incredible," I breathed, my eyes switching from his hands back to his face. "How did you *do* that?"

"It felt... natural," he explained.

Shaking my head, feeling incredibly insignificant, I replied, "What else can you do?"

With a wicked grin, Hugh glanced to the lighthouse, now visible down a stretch of sand. Across an open expanse of water, not far off from the sand bar was another lighthouse, extending out from the strip of land in Superior, known as Wisconsin Point. Between the two, large ships from the lake would gain access to the docks in Wisconsin.

"Do you trust me?" Hugh asked.

Letting out a breath, I answered, "Yes."

Before I realized he'd moved, Hugh whipped me into his arms, cradling me like a baby. The shriek of surprise was quickly cut off as we began to move.

What felt like a split second later, Hugh was setting me on my feet at the base of the lighthouse, which was about a mile from where we had just stood.

My knees gave out as I attempted to hold my weight, and Hugh's arms wrapped securely around my waist to assist.

As I strained to focus, I felt as if I were cross-eyed, having difficulty adjusting to the supernatural speed Hugh had just exhibited.

"What... what...."

His smile lit up once again, enjoying my befuddlement.

"You asked," he pointed out.

"Yeah, but... wow, that was so cool," I finally admitted.

He continued to anchor me as I took a look up at the lighthouse, then across the short expanse of water to the Wisconsin lighthouse. We had a pretty spectacular view from here, and I took deep breaths of the fresh air, the sun warming my skin.

Of course, my skin heating up might have had more to do with the man pressed tightly against me than the sun in the sky.

In the distance, I spotted several ships sitting out in the main lake, but one was headed our direction. With bated breath I watched as it approached, steering its way through the channel before us.

"Oh, awesome," I commented as it neared.

This was one of the larger ships, a thousand feet in length. As it approached, I had to crane my neck to see up to the railing.

As the machine was expertly maneuvered through the opening, I relaxed into Hugh's arms, feeling completely content.

We both watched silently until the ship made its way to a dock. Once it did, I turned to face Hugh directly.

"Let's go back to the beach," I said. "Will you carry me again?"

"Absolutely," he grinned, needing no more encouragement to scoop me into his arms.

Next thing I knew, my bare feet hit the sand, right on the water's edge. I stared down at my feet, then over to our discarded shoes, safely out of reach of the cool water.

I didn't think Hugh would ever cease to amaze me.

Giving myself a minute to be steady on my feet, I took a few steps into the lake, allowing the waves to wash over my feet and up to my ankles. The lake was calm today, and cold as always, though it felt refreshing in the sun. I knew from experience the gently moving water could create waves upwards of 20 feet, and my dad had once told me during extreme storms, they'd been recorded up to 30 feet.

It was no wonder this lake had once been mistaken for an ocean.

Hugh stood beside me, the water caressing his feet seeming to ground him. From our vantage point, we could see no other people- the popular swimming beach was a few miles down, and while the trail we'd walked was well used, few ventured this far down.

"What do you think that language was, in the memory? It made sense at the time, but now I can't remember any of the words."

"It seemed like it was a spell," Hugh said, his brows knitting. "Dominic mentioned an Elemental language– maybe that's what I was speaking."

It made as much sense as anything else.

"May I ask you about your last name?" Hugh asked, almost formally. "Though you didn't know your father growing up, you still have his name."

Nodding, I looked out over the gentle waves.

"I think my mom gave me his name, so that if I ever wanted, I could find him."

"I'm sorry I won't be able to meet her," Hugh said.

Glancing down, I linked my hand with Hugh's, meeting his gaze with my own. It was getting more and more difficult to deny any connection between us the longer we spent in each other's company. Perhaps, when something fit so seamlessly, it didn't matter how long we'd known one another.

"So am I. And, I want you to know, even with all the strangeness over the last few days, they've also been the best few days of my life," I told Hugh, laying myself on the line.

"Even though I can't remember anything besides the last few days, I have a feeling I wholeheartedly agree," Hugh smiled back.

We turned then, and after scooping up our shoes, began our walk back.

Chapter 13

The restaurant downtown we decided to meet Jade, Talon and Pearl at offered an array of burgers, fish and other local delicacies such as fried cheese curds. It also had a rooftop dining area, where we procured a table large enough to fit the five of us, plus my dad.

Pearl was flush with shopping bags, plopping into a chair with a huge grin. Jade's only carry-on was a camera bag, while Talon looked downright exhausted, and I understood completely.

"There are so many cute shops down here," Pearl said happily. "You missed out, Kate."

Exchanging a look with Jade, I answered, "I think I'm good."

"I've also gotten some amazing shots," Jade chimed in. "The lake, the boats and the bridges are excellent fodder. Not to mention all the old buildings."

"What did you two do?" Pearl asked with a sly smile.

Ignoring her double entendre, I replied, "Hiked on Park Point, down to the lighthouse. We managed to catch one of the ships coming into harbor, too."

My dad arrived then, and we placed our drink orders. Conversation flowed surprisingly easily, and I felt myself relaxing.

As we got ready to leave, my dad gave me a long hug.

"Good to see you, kid," he whispered into my ear.

"You too, Dad," I answered.

Pulling back, gripping my shoulders gently, my dad looked me in the eye and told me, "I like him. You've got yourself a good man there."

Nodding, I replied, "I think so, too."

"Call me when you get to California. I love you."

Wrapping my arms around his back once more, I answered, "I love you, too."

Hugh approached us as we parted, reaching out to shake my dad's hand.

"Harris, it was a pleasure to meet you," Hugh said.

"You, too," my dad answered. "I have a feeling we'll be seeing each other again."

With a glance at me, Hugh smiled. "I certainly hope so."

We clasped hands and watched my dad walk to his car, then meandered to our own. After getting back to the hotel, we said a brief goodnight to Jade, Talon and Pearl. I was exhausted again, and knew I would need a good night's sleep before heading out in the morning.

As I was pulling on my pajamas, there was a light knock on the door. Hugh answered for me, and I could hear Jade's voice through the bathroom door.

"I just wanted to go over the plan for the next few days," Jade said. "And, I was wondering if you'd like to try another session."

When I walked out, Hugh looked to me before answering. "I think it would be best to rest tonight, but I would like to try again tomorrow."

Smiling, Jade responded, "No problem. Where were you thinking of stopping tomorrow, Kate?"

"Somewhere in North Dakota or Montana," I told her. "Depending how far I got."

Her eyes lit up. "There's a State Park in Montana that I've been wanting to hit. It's right across the border of North Dakota, so I think it would be a perfect place to stop."

Shrugging, I answered, "Sure, sounds good."

"Yay!" Jade clapped her hands together giddily. "I have to make sure my camera batteries are charged."

Chuckling, I stifled a yawn. Jade was quick to notice.

"I'll let you get some rest. We'll be ready to go when you are."

"Thanks, Jade. Have a good night."

She left, and I made myself comfortable atop one of the beds. Hugh pulled off his shirt, and I was suddenly very attentive. He caught me staring, and a slow smile lit his face.

"Would you prefer I change in the bathroom?"

"Oh no, this is fine. Perfectly fine..." I trailed off, my eyes tracing down each perfectly chiseled muscle. "Man, you're good looking."

He laughed, sounding carefree. "Do you always get this blunt when you're tired?"

Rolling my eyes, I slid down on my side, bunching the pillow under my head as I continued to watch him.

"Seriously, though. You could be in one of those stripper dance shows."

"You attend many of these… stripper dance shows?"

Yawning, I shook my head. "No. Just see the advertisements."

"Well, it's good to know I have career options. Pit crew, stripper show…"

Smiling lazily, I commented, "I wonder what you really do for a living. I mean, not just anyone can run around shutting down torture camps. Were you some kind of law enforcement? CIA? Or you really are Batman…"

Chuckling again, Hugh turned off the lights and lay beside me. We faced each other in the dark, his heat seeping into my skin.

"Whatever it was, it will either come back to me or it won't. If not, I will find something new."

My eyes slid closed, sleep tugging at my consciousness.

Hugh's arm wrapped around my back, pulling me close. Nuzzling into the crook of his neck, I fell soundly into sleep.

111

*W*e rose bright and early, eager to be on our way. Talon and Jade were ready as promised- the revelation that they rarely slept was a tough one to swallow- and Pearl met us in the dining room to grab breakfast and say our goodbyes.

With my travel mug filled with hotel coffee, I wrapped my arms around my younger cousin.

"Oh, promise to come visit soon!" Pearl begged, tears lining her eyes.

"Of course! I'll be back for the weddings, at the very least," I winked at her, making her laugh.

"If you're waiting for Jade, it might be a few years! Make sure you come back for the reunion next summer."

"I'll do my best," I promised.

Pearl hugged Hugh next, whispering something into his ear that I couldn't quite hear. Hugh nodded seriously at her before turning to me.

"Take care of those kids, and give them hugs and kisses from me," I told her.

"You got it," Pearl grinned before hugging Jade, then Talon.

"You take care of my sister," she said sternly, waving a finger at him. "Or I'll tell Ella on you."

"Bringing out the big guns," Talon grumbled. Snagging Jade around the waist, he nodded solemnly. "I will always put Jade's safety first."

In response, Jade rolled her eyes dramatically. "He forgets, I can take care of myself."

Talon smiled indulgently, planting a kiss on Jade that deepened until we all looked away in embarrassment. When Talon finally released her, Jade blinked in a daze and nearly tripped over her own feet.

"You were saying?" he asked smugly, crossing his arms as she stumbled.

"You'll pay for that, wolf boy," Jade shot back, narrowing her eyes.

They both had goofy smiles on their faces, though, and I had to clear my throat to remind them that they still had company.

Jade gave us a guilty smile, leaning into Talon's side. He automatically wrapped an arm around her waist; they were always so in tune with each other. Even with all the ribbing, love shined between them like the brightest star.

"All right, let's get a move on," I encouraged. "We've got a long way to go today."

"Oh, I wish I could come with you guys," Pearl said. "But I also can't wait to get back to Micah and the kids. Call me every night to let me know where you are."

Jade promised she would, and we traipsed out to our cars.

Hugh and I climbed into my SUV, while Jade and Talon settled into a similar one. Jade had told me Talon's vehicle choice leaned more toward fast and expensive, but to help them blend in, especially in a town as small as Sun Valley, Jade had purchased the all-wheel drive vehicle.

It was also more comfortable for a road trip than, say, a two-door Porsche.

I led the way, setting us on a route that would lead us across Minnesota and through North Dakota.

The town we were headed for was a gateway to Makoshika State Park. It looked like a beautiful area, and I was hoping it would give Hugh an opportunity to test out his shifting abilities.

"Are you sad to leave your family?" Hugh asked quietly after several minutes of silence.

"A little," I admitted, "though having this large of a family is still new to me."

"It's nice," Hugh replied, a note of melancholy in his tone.

Risking a glance at his profile, I found his gaze downcast.

"We will find out your past," I promised him. "We'll find your family."

He nodded, reaching across to grip my hand. "Thank you. Not just for your words, but for everything. You helped a strange man who was bleeding to death in your trunk. Your capacity for love and understanding knows no bounds."

His words touched me, deep inside, and I felt myself slip just a bit more.

"With our connection, I don't know that I could have left you to your fate."

He shook his head in denial. "No, you would have helped me whether or not we were connected. Though, I must admit, I'm glad we are. I couldn't imagine a better person to be tied to."

"If you keep talking like this, I'm going to be forced to pull the car over and kiss you," I warned.

His smile grew, forcing the darkness away. It took my breath, and I had to compel myself to pay attention to the road.

Chapter 14

After checking in at the hotel, we decided to grab a pizza-
actually, make that two pizzas, since Jade was with us-
and eat in the room so we could talk.

After my first two slices, I was full. Hugh and I were perched on the edge of the bed again, while Talon and Jade made use of the small dinette.

Jade was studying me with an expression I recognized- she had an idea.

"What is it?" I asked.

"I was just thinking... have you tried to tap into your ability? I'm curious what else you'd be able to do with it."

"What do you mean?"

She relaxed back, pausing in her eating, to explain further. "When I discovered I was an empath, I didn't really know what that meant. The basics of it is reading other's emotions, or even taking them upon myself. The first time I connected to another's memories was by complete accident."

Talon shifted in his seat. "She neglects to mention how dangerous that event was."

Jade smirked at her fiancé before continuing her train of thought. "I just think you have a lot of untapped potential."

"Something to think about," I acknowledged. "How would I even begin testing it?"

Thinking this through, Jade struggled to explain. "When I connect to someone, I close my eyes and imagine their aura. Talon, for instance, is full of earthy tones, browns and deep reds, while yours is bright, like a pure white. Those colors become strands, and I latch onto one and allow it to pull me into their mind."

Digesting that information, I shrugged my shoulders before turning to Hugh. "I'm game."

He nodded. "I'll be your guinea pig."

Closing my eyes, I focused on Hugh's colors, picturing them the way Jade explained. I imagined he would be dark colors, black and gray, but with a hint of gold.

Popping one eye open, I glanced around the room before admitting defeat. "Nothing happened."

Jade laughed lightly. "You were only trying for 30 seconds. Try again."

Pursing my lips, I closed my eyes again. This time I really concentrated, reaching out with a hand to grasp at the strands.

At hearing Jade's muffled laughter, I opened both my eyes wide. "What?"

"I'm sorry," Jade giggled. "You were acting it out."

Letting out a breath, I threw up my hands in defeat. "That's it, I'm done."

"No, no don't do that," Jade pleaded.

Hugh cleared his throat, amused by our exchange but wanting to bring up an idea.

"When you first told me about your ability, you mentioned that it came out when people pushed you. What if it's emotion based?"

"Interesting," Talon sat forward, intrigued now. "Shall we yell at you?"

We all grinned, but Hugh was the one to answer.

"No, I think we need to go the opposite way," Hugh interjected. "When people push at you, you've always pushed back. Now, you're trying to pull someone toward you."

He turned to me. *Close your eyes.*

I did as he directed.

This time, instead of speaking, he sent me impressions of images. The way if felt when his hands wrapped around my waist. The joy of watching me sleep, the way I would sigh a little and scoot into his heat. The brush of his lips against my temple, my cheek, my lips. The way my blood sang as his teeth nipped against my neck.

Streams of light began to dance behind my lids, shimmering golds like the hour of sunset. They weren't strands, so much as playful waves, reaching out to envelop me in their warmth. Willingly, eagerly, I stepped into the light.

Hugh's form shimmered into view, though his outline was indistinct. There was something different about him, and I studied his features, traced each line of his face until I realized the difference.

The stress of the world was gone from his eyes, as they were shining clearly at me. His lips moved easily into a smile, where so much of the time it seemed forced. His hand moved fluidly to cup my cheek, a gesture I associated now with the man I'd fallen so hard for.

No words passed between us- they didn't need to. In the moment, there was a complete, total understanding between our souls.

With a gasp, I realized the truth of that statement. This was the embodiment of Hugh's soul, the golden hue revealing his true self. I'd been wrong about the dark aura- Hugh was a shimmering light, like water sprinkled with rays of light at the hour of sunset. Away from the darkness of the world, he shone like a beacon on the darkest night.

My eyes opened to meet his, the golden wash of light still encompassing our forms. In that instant, I knew the truth.

I was hopelessly in love with Hugh, and he was my mate.

My hand reached out, glowing softly in its own pure white, and came to rest against his chest. A million thoughts passed between us in an instant. Our lights fused together, and there were no secrets between us. Our souls were laid bare; I was his, and he was mine.

Blinking once, the world snapped back into focus. Hugh and I let out a breath simultaneously, unable to look anywhere but each other.

Jade let out a sigh. "I guess it didn't work."

Forcing my gaze away from Hugh and to my cousin, I asked, "What do you mean?"

"You only had your eyes closed for a few seconds," she told me. "It's okay, it was just a thought."

Hugh and I exchanged an incredulous look.

"You saw that, right?" I asked him.

"Yes, I did," he answered.

"How long did that feel to you?"

He shook his head, searching for an answer. "Definitely longer than a few seconds."

"Wait, what are you saying? It worked?" Jade's voice rose in pitch to match her excitement.

Nodding, I switched my gaze back to her. "Big time."

"Tell me everything," she sat forward, eager now.

"I... well, I think I connected to his soul."

Talon and Jade's mouths dropped open, which was comical all on its own. But, given what Jade was capable of, I didn't know why they were so surprised.

Explaining what had just happened the best I could, leaving out my personal revelation, Talon tapped a finger against his chin before being the first one to speak.

"It's interesting, how your powers are related to Jade's. Your grandmother had the sight, and was able to read people through touch. Jade is an empath, able to feel or even take on other's emotions, and connect to their memories. You, Kate, you are able to manipulate other's emotions, and connect to their very soul."

"It's also interesting that when I've connected to memories, to me, it feels like a short time has passed when in reality it could have been hours, while yours is the opposite," Jade added.

It took me a moment to process all this, and formulate a response. Talon spoke of Grandma Stryder, whom I'd only met briefly during the reunion. Jade had mentioned she was also Gifted, but we hadn't had a chance to go into detail.

"Manipulating emotions," I finally murmured. "That sounds like a dangerous ability."

"In the wrong hands, perhaps," Talon agreed. "But, I believe you will only use it for good."

This was sounding more and more like a superhero movie. If Hugh was Batman, who was I? Probably one of the X-Men.

Great, now we're not even in the same universe.

Needing a distraction, I asked, "You said all Elementals are able to manipulate the elements; earth, wind, fire and water. They're able to shapeshift, and drink blood to survive. What else is similar? And does everyone have a bonus gift, like Jade and I?"

Talon chuckled at the phrase 'bonus gift,' before answering. "Depending how you look at it, shapeshifting is just another element manipulation. Many recognize spirit, or akasha, as the fifth element. But, to answer your question, I suppose the other main similarities are the fact that we don't really need sleep..."

"Except to heal, and we'll get groggy for a few hours in the afternoon," Jade interrupted.

"And our longevity," Talon finished.

I was almost afraid to ask. "Longevity?"

"Though we are, under extreme circumstances, able to be killed... we are, for all intents and purposes, immortal."

Drawing in a breath, I glanced to Hugh. His wide eyes met mine as the same thought raced through both our minds.

How old was he?

Turning to Talon, I asked, "So, how old are you?"

He laughed, "Am I getting wrinkles?"

Jade nudged him. "Go on, tell her."

"I was raised by my mother and father, in the land that is now known as New Mexico. We were part of the Apache people, before the Europeans laid claim to the land."

"You mean you were born in the fifteen *hundreds*?" My jaw hung open in shock.

"Roughly 1520," Talon confirmed. Watching my face carefully, he continued, "As for your second question, I'm not sure if everyone has a 'bonus' gift, but it seems as if most of us do. You and Jade, for example. Our friend Lani is able to speak telepathically to animals— which includes Elementals, when we're in animal form— and I'm a gem caller."

"Gem caller?" My brows knit at the unfamiliar term.

"I'm very closely attuned to the earth, more so than others of our kind. Just as it sounds, I am able to find specific materials, by asking the earth where to locate them. While I grew up living off the land and had no use for money, I have found it easier to navigate the modern world, and so I used my ability to create a thriving business. That is, until I realized where I needed to be to find my soul mate."

At this, Talon raised Jade's hand to his mouth and placed a sweet kiss on her palm. To my amusement, pink color rose in Jade's cheeks as she smiled at the floor.

Jade held out her left hand, showing off her unusual, yet gorgeous engagement ring. The chunk of turquoise was surrounded by glittering diamonds, set into a platinum band.

"This is some of his handiwork," she explained. "And, might I say, my favorite."

Talon's grin showed off his dimples, and in that moment, it was difficult for me to see the centuries old, powerful creature that he truly was.

"Are you all right? This is a lot of information to process," Talon seemed concerned.

"It is, but I'm fine. Hugh? Has any of this triggered your memories?"

He shook his head, directing his answer at Talon. "Not yet, but I am curious about shapeshifting. Do you think you could walk me through it?"

"I'd be happy to," Talon replied.

Chapter 15

The four of us gathered in a small clearing in the badlands, lit only by the soft glow of the half moon. Though Hugh was concerned for my safety, I made the very compelling argument that I was the reason shadowmen were unable to find him, and so I was going to remain by his side for the foreseeable future.

Jade and I did stand off to the side, giving the men plenty of space for practicing shapeshifting. She had a camera around her neck, hoping to get some night shots of the beautiful park.

Gray ridges of hardened sand jutted into the sky while coppery boulders balanced precariously on wind-torn perches. The place had an overall feeling of mystery; a perfect setting for our men to practice such an otherworldly talent as shapeshifting.

"We normally begin nude," Talon began, then sent us a wary glance. "Er, ladies? Would you mind turning away?"

"So shy all of a sudden," Jade murmured, laughter bubbling up. Louder, she said, "Sure thing, hot stuff. We'll protect your delicate sensibilities."

Talon's gaze darkened, and I had a feeling more passed between them through their telepathic link. Jade continued to chuckle as we turned away, looking out over the exposed bluffs with layer upon layer of prehistoric stone.

"What did he say?" I whispered, knowing very well all three could hear me.

"He promised retribution," she smirked, clearly fine with the idea.

Letting out a small laugh, I listened closely to Talon's instructions. Though I wanted to share the experience with Hugh, Jade had warned me not to speak to him, whether out loud or through our link, as it took such complete concentration to transform.

Once the men had dropped their clothes in piles, Talon began to instruct.

"Close your eyes, and clear your mind. Breathe deep, and let all thoughts, all worries, go. When you've done this, picture a wolf. Fill your mind's eye with the creature- the shape of its eyes, the length of its fur. The way it smells, the way it thinks. Every detail, down to the nails on each paw."

The air shimmered with a distinct power, and I knew, without a doubt, that I would turn to find a wolf.

Jade motioned for me to turn, knowing that Talon had also completed his transformation, and my breath caught as I took in the site of the large, black wolf closest to me.

Looking at the chocolate eyes, it was obvious to me that this was Talon. He turned his head toward the second figure, and my gaze shot past him to land on Hugh.

I would recognize him in any form. His wolf was as large as Talon's, with sleek, dark gray fur. When his eyes met mine, I found the same glittering deep brown that I'd come to know so well.

His mouth split open and his tongue lolled out in a wolfy grin. Before I realized his intention, Hugh launched himself at me.

He stopped at my feet, pressing against my legs. Sinking my hands into his thick fur, I felt a pleasant rumble reverberating from his throat.

"You're gorgeous," I breathed, unable to take my eyes off him.

Dropping to my knees, I allowed his head to nuzzle mine. Then, his large, wet tongue shot out and licked my face from chin to temple.

Pulling back with a laugh, I wiped at the goo and groaned. "Aw, gross."

He leapt away, the same grin and sudden light-heartedness preventing me from truly being upset.

"Oh, go, you mangy mutt," I winked, watching as he loped off into the night, Talon at his heals. To Jade I said, "That is so cool."

"It really is," she agreed. "I've been wanting to ask, but we haven't had a moment alone. You realize that you could become an Elemental, right?"

Letting out a breath, I answered, "Yes."

"Well?" she asked, eyebrows raised. "Have you thought about it?"

"Jade... I've only known Hugh a short time. Days. Making a lifelong commitment..."

She held out her hands, palms toward me. "Say no more. It took Talon weeks to convince me just to date him. But, learn from my mistakes. When it's right, it's right. You obviously feel the connection to Hugh, and vice versa."

"Yeah," I sighed. "That's undeniable."

Jade shrugged, looking back toward the direction the boys had taken off. "Just something to think about."

"What made you decide to change?"

Though she tried to stop the wince, I caught it anyway. "I had basically made up my mind, though Talon was resistant. He was going to give up his powers to age with me. But then, Gerry shot me, and it was the only way he could save my life."

"Wow," I breathed. Though I'd heard the story of Gerry's flip out, Jade and Talon had obviously done a good job covering the extent of it. "Do you regret it?"

"No," Jade told me. "Every moment I spend with Talon is a gift. The fact that I have an eternity of those moments is breathtaking. I know we'll have some issues to deal with, like the fact that we won't age while the rest of my family does, but we'll figure out a way to deal with that together."

I was silent for a while, thinking through what Jade had said. When I finally answered, I could just see a glimpse of two dark figures in the distance, coming back to us.

"I don't think I can make any decisions until Hugh has his memory back," I said. "Until then, the future is a big question mark."

"Totally understandable. If he's up for it, I'd like to try another session tonight."

The wolves skidded to a stop, panting from their run.

"Before you change back, could you become mountain lions?" Jade called out, holding up her camera. "They're more indigenous to this area than wolves."

This time, I got to watch the transformation. The wolves shimmered into nothingness before reconnecting in the form of mountain lions. I let out a huff of breath, amazed by the sight in front of me.

I watched with amusement as Jade posed two seemingly wild animals for some beautiful photos. It was obvious this wasn't the first time she'd convinced Talon to be her model- albeit in animal form.

When she was content with her photos, they stood and stared at us until Jade smirked and turned around, gesturing for me to do the same.

That same shimmer in the air could be felt as they returned to their natural forms. We waited a little longer to allow them to dress, and turned when Talon spoke.

"You were a natural," Talon complimented Hugh.

When I turned to face him, Hugh was within a few feet. He took my hand as the wide smile remained in place.

"That was incredible," he told me excitedly.

My own smile lit my eyes, the growing love I felt for him shining out plainly for all to see.

"Let's go back to the hotel," I said breathily, surprised by the quality of my own voice. It was deep... and seductive.

"I think we'll stay a while," Jade told us, taking the hint. "I'd like to take a run, too."

Nodding, I bid them goodnight before allowing Hugh to lift me in his arms. He slipped into our room, and didn't relinquish his hold. My arms were around his neck, my eyes on his. Leaning in, I met his lips with mine.

Hugh kissed me back, long and thorough. When I finally came up for a breath, the golden hue of his aura was shining brightly. In complete understanding, Hugh walked to the bed and laid me in the middle, sliding to his side beside me.

His hand cupped my cheek as he stared deeply into my eyes. Our connection was more than physical, more than emotional. Our very souls blended together so seamlessly it was difficult to tell where he left off and I began.

"I love you, Kate," Hugh said softly.

"I love you, too," I replied, pouring everything I felt in that moment into our next kiss.

His hands began to explore, gentle but sure. The fire sparked and grew, engulfing us both as each kiss, every touch became more urgent.

Hugh's hand splayed across my stomach, pulling his head back to meet my eyes. My body was a raging fire; a blaze only Hugh could quench.

"You're certain?" he asked gently.

"Yes. You're my mate, and I love you. I want you. Every part of you," I replied with utter honesty.

His mouth dipped back to mine with something akin to a growl. Though it was in his very nature to be dominant, he displayed nothing but tenderness. With his hands and his mouth, he worked me expertly to a fever pitch. Only when my mind cried out for him did he join us together, and my body spiraled out with that first delicious release.

Though it must have taken every ounce of control he contained, Hugh continued to move slow and gentle, bringing me to the edge once again. His teeth nipped along my neck, and my head arched back in offering.

Take what is yours, I sent into his mind. *I offer freely.*

The words came unbidden to my thoughts, but they felt right. Unable to resist the lure of his mate, Hugh's fangs lengthened and pricked the sensitive skin just below my jaw.

The initial pain quickly gave way to a pleasure unlike anything I ever could have imagined. Hugh's gentle suckling spun me out of control and we fell together, spinning off the ledge and into the stars.

Chapter 16

I was teetering in that hazy moment between dream and wake; my body rested on a cloud, warm and soft, while gentle lips prodded me back to consciousness.

"Good morning," Hugh said, his voice a husky thread of sound.

Curling into his warmth, I murmured, "Mm, good morning."

"You're so beautiful when you sleep," Hugh observed, running his fingers through my hair. "Your hair splays out over the pillow, and you look so peaceful."

His lips trailed from my temple to the upward curve of my lips.

"Of course, nothing rivals the beauty of the intelligence sparking in those emerald eyes."

At this, I lifted my lashes to find Hugh watching me. My heart skipped a beat at the look in his eyes, a look that laid bare all his feelings for me.

"You are one sweet talker," I commented.

"It's easy when I speak the truth," he grinned, that little boy's smile completely disarming me.

Lifting my head to meet his lips, I realized just how sore I was in places that I'd never been sore before. I let out a little groan, and it snagged Hugh's attention immediately.

"What's wrong?" he asked, pulling away to check me over.

"Nothing," I reassured him. "Just a little... sore."

Regret instantly marred his face. "I'm so sorry."

Laughter bubbled up, and I trapped his face between my palms. "It's a good sore, trust me."

Lifting my head, I sniffed and rose a brow, effectively changing the subject.

"Do I smell coffee?"

Hugh shook his head, amused by my antics. "What my woman wants, my woman gets."

Swiftly rolling to his feet, Hugh snagged two mugs from the small dinette and brought them back to the bed. I scooted against the frame, accepting the cup as he held it out to me.

"A girl could get used to this," I said, inhaling the steam before taking a sip.

"If it means waking up next to you, I will gladly bring you coffee every morning."

"Speaking of," I paused, taking another sip. "Jade said last night that you really don't need sleep, except to heal. Does that mean you've been awake all night?"

"Not all night," Hugh defended. "I think I've been able to sleep since my mind is in need of healing."

"I've always had trouble sleeping at night," I confided. "When I'm able to set my own hours, I usually sleep in the afternoon. Maybe that's because I'm Gifted?"

"Could be," Hugh nodded. "And, if that's the schedule you prefer, it will certainly make things easier in the future."

Nodding, I kept my other thoughts to myself. Jade's question when we'd been alone had been nagging at the back of my mind, but I set any decisions aside for the moment. Right now, I wanted to enjoy the time with Hugh– and then we had to get back on the road.

We showered together– which quickly led to distraction– and dressed before heading down with our bags. Jade and Talon were just coming back in, both bogged down with camera equipment.

"The sun rising over the badlands was incredible," Jade grinned, giving me a once over. "You look... refreshed."

Annoyingly, I felt a blush creep up my neck and settle into my cheeks.

"I slept well," I told her before turning to the dining room. "Let's eat, I'm starved."

While we ate our fill of waffles and omelet's, Jade received a phone call.

"It's Reese," she said aloud, before answering.

Even with my human hearing, I could tell it was a man's voice, not Reese's on the other end.

Jade's eyes widened as she listened, and asked, "Is there anything we can do?"

Whatever the response was, she nodded along. Talon and Hugh's countenance had darkened, and I was instantly worried for Reese.

"All right, keep us in the loop. We'll come back if needed."

"What's going on?" I asked immediately.

"It's Reese... she's going through the conversion," Jade answered before explaining further. "She was taken by a shadowman. Dominic went to rescue her, and the shadowman got the upper hand. He was knocked unconscious, and when he woke, they were in a small building that was on fire. Reese had cut open a wound on her wrist to heal Dominic– she was secured to the ground and couldn't escape."

"So, he saved her," I breathed, my heart in my throat. "Is she all right? Will she be all right, I mean?"

"I think so. The conversion can do wonders," Jade answered, reaching across and squeezing Talon's knee. "We know that first hand."

"Can we help?" I asked.

"Dominic said he has it covered, but that he'll keep us updated."

The conversation had turned us all melancholy, but there was nothing to do but move forward.

We hit the road once again. Our next destination was on the border of Idaho and Nevada; it was about a ten-hour drive, and one of the last places to stop if we didn't want to drive all the way to Reno. Tomorrow, we would make the final leg of the trip.

Talon had told us of a piece of property he owned northeast of San Francisco– it would be a good place to stay until my condo was ready. He told us the home was secluded, and would give us an opportunity to help Hugh with his memories and practice his other Elemental skills.

When we reached the hotel in Twin Falls, we grabbed a quick dinner before gathering in our room. Since we hadn't delved into Hugh's memory the night before, Jade wanted to give it a try.

We sat comfortably on opposite beds. Jade closed her eyes to concentrate, while I wrapped my hand around Hugh's for support. I knew, from the first time we'd tried this, that it could be an hour or more before they came back to this reality.

Waiting patiently, I allowed my mind to wander through different possibilities for the future; if Hugh's memory didn't return, would that change my decisions?

In the midst of all the uncertainty, there was one thing I knew without a doubt; Hugh and I were meant to be together.

Jade's eyes blinked open first, taking a few moments to re-assimilate to the present. I watched Hugh as his eyes opened, unfocused at first.

"Were you able to see anything?" I asked.

With a tentative smile, he nodded. "Yes. I saw my brother. We were young, and playing in a garden– the same garden we saw for a moment in the other memory."

His eyes softened as he reached out to tug gently on the ends of my hair.

"It was filled with kakabeak flowers."

His action warmed me, and I smiled back. "Do you know where you were?"

"It was our home," he said, "but as for a location, I'm still not sure."

"It was beautiful," Jade piped in. "A big white house, lots of land. Not like anything I've seen. You said kakabeak flower... what is that?"

"It's a flower indigenous to New Zealand," I explained. "It was one of Hugh's first memories."

Jade pondered this information before nodding. "That could have been New Zealand."

"It was the same house as the memory you helped me unlock," Hugh said.

"And if you have a brother out there, we'll find him," I promised.

"A twin brother," Jade added. "Which, I hear, is typical of Elementals."

"Good to know," I murmured.

I was excited to reach our destination– not only was Talon's property nestled into the mountains, but I was getting a little tired of being cooped up in the car every day.

We pulled onto the dirt drive leading to the home in the picturesque setting. The cabin, as Talon called it, was actually a sprawling mansion, built into the mountain itself. The front of the house was covered in floor to ceiling windows, with several multi-tiered patios.

Off to the side, there was a large, flat field with a few outbuildings. The patios overlooked the Trinity River, which flowed erratically through the ravine.

"Holy crap, Talon," I exclaimed as we got out of our vehicles. "This place is gorgeous."

He shrugged casually. "I own several properties over the world. They come in useful when you live such a long time."

While I gawked at him, Jade was whipping out her camera. "I can't believe we haven't been here yet. This is amazing."

"Why don't you ladies take a look around, and we'll bring the bags inside?" Talon offered.

"Deal!" Jade grinned, grabbing my arm and pulling me along.

Sending Hugh a smirk over my shoulder, I followed her lead. We ventured out onto a mountain path, taking in the sweeping views of the Shasta-Trinity mountain range.

The sun was sinking in the sky as we trekked along, washing the entire valley in a warm, coppery red hue.

"Almost makes me want to stay here," Jade observed, her camera down for the moment as she simply enjoyed the view. "Could you ever get used to this?"

"I'm not sure," I answered. "But I wouldn't mind giving it a try."

We turned then to head back toward the cabin, when an uneasy feeling slid along my skin. Jade and I both paused, sharing a look of complete understanding.

Huge, winged shadows descended upon us, and before I could even shout for Hugh in my mind, three figures appeared before us.

Three very familiar figures. They were the same creatures that had attacked Hugh and I when we'd gotten a flat tire.

I opened my mouth to command them, when the man in the middle wove his hands in a complicated pattern and intoned a spell. Though I tried, no words came from my lips.

"We learned from last time," the man smirked. "Now, you will come with us."

I tried to move, whether forward to attack or backward to run, but my limbs were rooted to the ground.

Hugh! I called out in my mind, as the shadowman approached me. He murmured another incantation, and the whole world faded to black.

Chapter 17

Consciousness returned with a vicious reminder of my current predicament. My cheek rested against a cold, hard ground, and my entire body ached. Knowing I wasn't alone, I remained completely still.

Hugh? I sent out, and immediately winced as a sharp pain blocked my attempt at telepathy. The shadowmen must have used more spells to block communication.

With no concept of how much time had passed, I knew I had to act fast if I wanted to get out of this situation. The original spells seemed to have worn off- the use of my vocal chords returned. Slipping my eyes open a slit, I took in as much of my surroundings as possible without giving myself away.

I was alone in a cell, with a single shadowman as my guard. It was the man with the teal eyes and long, jet black hair who had lifted me into the air back in Wisconsin.

Summoning all my power, I spoke without bothering to stand. "Don't move."

The shadowman stilled, his eyes wide with shock.

"Tell me your name," I commanded, pushing myself to my feet.

Though the creature flinched, he couldn't deny my request. "Lucius. Lucius Nicolette."

"What do you want with me?" Using the same tone, I left no room for Lucius to evade.

"I'm looking for my mate. She can give me my soul back."

"Do you believe I'm your mate?" I asked softly.

He shuddered, fighting some inner demon before responding. "No. But you will be."

I shook my head slowly, feeling sorry for this creature who was once a great man. "No, I won't be. My mate is out there, and there's only one for each of us. No matter what you say or do to me, I will never forget him."

Lucius remained rigid. His eyes bore into mine, and I allowed him to see the truth of my statement.

Using my power again, I said, "There must be some good in you. Search deep. Find that goodness, and latch on. Clear away the darkness. Be the man I know you can be."

He jerked back like he'd been struck, his eyes squeezing tight as his fists pressed against his temples.

"Lucius," I called out. "Lucius, look at me!"

His eyes popped open, panting with the effort of fighting my commands.

Though I'd only attempted this with Hugh, I took a deep breath and made the plunge. Keeping my eyes on Lucius, ensnaring him with my gaze, I opened myself up to the love I felt for Hugh.

Anger fueled my words; love fueled my connection to another. When I connected to Hugh, his soul shined with the most gorgeous golden hues. As Lucius' soul lay bare for me, it was a very different story.

The waves of dark light were made up of a crimson so dark it was nearly black. Though I couldn't see his memories like Jade, to understand how he had come to this point, I could clearly see the aftermath.

I reached out with a hand, tears stinging my eyes at the utter devastation before me. Where my fingers touched the edge of his light, it recoiled, afraid of the pure white.

I allowed my hand to hover there, showing no ill will. The crimson waves kept their distance, as if they were waiting for me to strike.

"It's okay," I found myself saying. "I'm here to help. Show me you want to be good."

The smallest tendril reached out, sliding against my light with a tentative touch. A cool breeze slid along my skin, the sudden icy chill of darkness leaving goosebumps along my arms.

"That's the way," I coaxed the crimson. "Join me. Leave the darkness behind."

There was a heavy silence, an endless moment of suspended motion. Then, suddenly, our lights collided, shining bright as an exploding star. The force of it knocked me on my back, and I came back to reality with a gasp.

Propping myself up on my elbows, I squinted through the bars to the outside room, where Lucius lay sprawled on the floor. Though I was dizzy, I forced myself to my feet.

On shaking legs, I gripped the bars and called out to the unconscious man.

"Lucius! Wake up! Lucius!"

His head moved, rolling from one side to another. A low groan came from his throat, so I knew he was alive.

"Lucius! Are you all right?"

His eyes slid open, glazed in pain. They locked on me, and his mouth sucked in a breath.

"Kate," he said, his voice gruff. "What... what happened?"

This was not the same man who had kidnapped me. Hope blossomed in my chest.

"How do you feel?" I asked in place of answering his question.

"My head... I feel... funny," he ended, sitting up gingerly with a palm to his forehead. "I feel... different."

"Do you remember bringing me here?"

He shook his head as if clearing it. "Yes... no... I mean, I do, but the memory is fuzzy. Why would I do this to you?"

Lifting himself to his feet, Lucius approached me slowly. Taking out the key, he slipped it into the lock before murmuring a few words to break the spell holding me inside.

I backed away, waiting for him to open the door.

"Thank you," I breathed, inspecting him to be sure he hadn't received any physical harm. "We need to save my friends. Will you help me?"

"Of course," he murmured, his eyes soft on mine. "Anything for you."

Uh-oh. Not having the time to worry about his unusual reaction toward me, I followed Lucius out of the building and into the next.

Jade was unconscious on the floor of her cell, another shadowman standing guard. He stared down at her with arms crossed, not bothering to look up as Lucius entered.

"Silas," Lucius acknowledged the other creature.

Silas turned, and, spotting me, immediately went into attack mode. Lucius wrapped one arm around Silas' throat, then wrangled the man's hands behind his back. They both faced me, Silas struggling wildly while Lucius watched me calmly.

"Do the same for him that you did for me," Lucius spoke conversationally, as if we had all the time in the world.

Taking a deep breath and ignoring the ragged beat of my heart, I looked squarely at Silas.

"Silas. Look at me."

Injecting my power into my voice, Silas had no option but to obey. I stepped closer, bolstered by my earlier success.

"There's a good man inside you, hidden deep. A good man that will be deserving of his mate. Reach inside yourself now and find him. Bring him to the surface."

Silas grunted and began twisting in earnest, the pain of facing his own demons almost too much to bear. Because of my earlier command, his eyes remained on mine, spitting fire.

"Stop this," he hissed out.

Shaking my head, I took another step forward. "No. I know there's good in you. Let's find it, together."

Giving in to my emotions was becoming easier with practice. My bright light shone out, bathing the men before me in its brilliance. As I took a brief moment to examine the waves rolling from me, I jolted with surprise at finding the lightest trace of pink, hovering along the feathery edge.

My gaze switched first to Silas, who was battling a deep, dark soul with just a hint of green, and over to Lucius.

Gone was the overall darkness— now, immediately surrounding his body was a beautiful pink hue, gradually darkening to crimson along the outer edges. Most curiously was the small, bright white hovering near his heart.

Tucking the information into the back of my mind, I turned my full attention to Silas, who was watching me with equal parts alarm and hope.

"It's all right," I told his emerald soul. "It's time to come back. I'm here for you. Join me."

Reaching out slowly, I allowed my light to mix with his. It didn't recoil as much as Lucius' had, and I wondered if the fact that Lucius was at Silas' back had anything to do with that fact. He was literally surrounded by goodness, with nowhere to retreat.

The dark emerald light swirled against mine, a mesmerizing dance of souls. When the moment of suspended animation struck, I braced myself for the explosion that knocked me off my feet.

Chapter 18

In the blink of an eye, Silas was lowered gently to the floor and I found myself cushioned from the rough concrete. I let out a breath, appreciative of the support, but realizing it was Lucius' arms wrapped around me.

Clearing my throat, I stood and took a step away from the man who had saved me from another fall.

"Thank you," I said quietly, then turned my attention to Jade. "Would you please get my cousin out of there?"

Lucius nodded, quick to do my bidding. I approached Silas, checking to be sure he was breathing.

"Silas? I need you to wake up. Silas!"

With a groan, his hand reached up and clasped mine against his chest.

"Kate," he muttered, still on the edge of consciousness.

"That's right," I told him. "I'm here. Open your eyes."

He struggled to do as I asked, his baby blues soft and wary.

"What happened?" he asked.

"It's a long story. Let's get you up."

While I helped Silas to his feet, I watched Lucius scoop Jade from the ground. She was still out for the count, and I rushed over to make sure she was still breathing.

"She will recover," Lucius promised. "She attempted to use her powers on Silas, but was blocked by the shield."

Another piece of information to tuck away for later. Nodding, I asked Lucius to show me to where Talon and Hugh were being held.

He led the way, though he allowed Silas to enter first. Both men were in a cell together, glaring daggers at the third shadowman.

Hugh and Talon saw us and immediately went slack-jawed. The third shadowman spun at the intrusion, set on attacking. Silas launched himself forward to protect me, and a full fist-fight broke out between them.

Lucius lay Jade carefully on the ground before joining the fray. With two against one, the third shadowman had no chance.

"Traitors! What is wrong with you! Let me go!"

"Look at me," I commanded, stepping close.

Behind the bars I saw Hugh and Talon both surge forward, protests at their lips. I held up a hand to them, letting them know I had this handled. I couldn't speak to Hugh telepathically, not while he was behind the shield the shadowmen had placed over the cell.

"What is your name?" I asked the creature, once I got his attention.

"Augustus," he ground out through his teeth, his jaw clenched tight. "Release me, woman."

"Augustus," I said quietly, "you are a good man. Somewhere, deep down, you've buried your goodness. I want you to uncover it now."

"No!" he shrieked, struggling against his captors.

"Augustus!" I called out over his cries. "Be the man your future mate deserves!"

Without another word, I allowed my love to take over, my white light now tinged with both a light pink and soft green. Dimly I registered Hugh's gasp as he saw the difference.

We were all connected in the room. Hugh, with his golden brilliance my steady anchor. Talon, with the deep browns of the desert. Jade, in varying shades of vibrant purple and teal. Lucius, with his odd ombré of pink to crimson. Silas, with a similar fading effect, the waves starting with just the lightest sea foam along his body, spiraling out to the darkest emerald along the edges.

Silas had the same small, strange white glow just above his heart. It remained steady even as the waves undulated.

My attention swiftly turned to Augustus, his dark blue, almost black soul quivering in fear.

"Join me," I spoke to him, to his soul. "Let's find your mate together. She's out there, waiting for you. Come back to goodness. Join me."

As before, I reached out with my light, caressing along the edges. Though the blue hue didn't recoil, it continued to shake, reminding me of a lost, beaten puppy.

"It's all right," I soothed. "No harm will come to you ever again."

Though the blue light didn't move closer, I sensed its acceptance. Still slowly, I moved closer, closing my light over the frightened soul.

The same moment of absolute silence hovered over the room, before the light explosion sent us all reeling back.

Lucius caught me again, cushioning my fall from the explosion of light. Silas lowered his friend to the ground, searching for signs of life. When my eyes opened they shot to Hugh, relief pouring off me in waves.

"Hugh," I murmured, the stress of the situation finally settling into my bones.

"Wait here," Lucius instructed softly, before rising and releasing the men from their prison.

Talon arrived at Jade's side in a split second, whispering to her tenderly. Hugh was beside me before I could blink, concern etched into his features.

"Are you all right? What was that?"

"I think we all have some things to talk about," I answered, my eyes landing on Augustus as he came back to consciousness. "Is there a safe place, away from here?"

I didn't want to volunteer the cabin without Talon's permission.

Hugh exchanged a glance with Talon before nodding. He lifted me to my feet, wrapping an arm around my waist. I leaned heavily into him, grateful for the ability to do so.

"I need to speak to Augustus," I said to Hugh, motioning with a nod of my head.

Hugh guided me to Silas and Augustus, who was just getting to his feet again.

"Are you all right?" I asked, concern marring my tone.

Hugh sent me a sharp look but said nothing.

"Yes. What happened? Why are we in this place?"

"We're going to have a long conversation, but first, we need to get somewhere safe. Will you three join us?"

"Of course," Silas said immediately.

"Yes," Augustus agreed.

"We will do anything for you, Kate," Lucius added.

Their almost reverent tone when they spoke to me was unnerving. Not just for me, but for Hugh as well.

I looked over to Talon, who had scooped Jade into his arms. Her eyes were open, yet glazed, but I was happy to see them.

"Lead the way, Talon," I smiled, wrapping my arms around Hugh's neck as he lifted me from my feet.

In a blink we were gone from the brick buildings that had been our prisons. While he ran, I nuzzled into Hugh's neck, breathing in his scent and allowing his warmth to revive me.

I love you, I sent into his mind.

For a moment, his run faltered and I could feel his racing pulse against my cheek. I wasn't the only one who was under stress.

You are everything to me, Kate, he responded.

And even though we were racing to an undisclosed location with three former shadowmen at our back, I'd never felt more at peace.

Chapter 19

Talon led us back to the cabin in the middle of the mountains, far from civilization. He immediately set to work at building a fire in the main living space, snuggling Jade into a large chair with a blanket wrapped around her form.

Sinking into a chair beside my cousin, I reached over and clasped her hand. It was chilly, which I'd come to realize was unusual for an Elemental. As when I'd first found Hugh, when his body temperature had lowered to fight blood loss, Jade's had lowered to fight the foreign spell that had downed her in the first place.

Hugh stood beside me, a possessive hand on my shoulder, while Talon stood protectively near Jade.

The three former shadowmen faced us, their handsome features restored now that the stench of evil had been removed.

I looked first to Lucius, with his startling teal eyes and long, jet black hair curling along his ears. Next, I studied Augustus, his eyes the color of wheat with specks of green grass, his long, dark brown hair clasped together low on his neck. Finally, my gaze settled on Silas, his short, close cropped and slightly spiky hair and baby blue eyes that watched me in return.

"Why don't we start with introductions?" I asked into the awkward silence. When no one spoke, I shrugged. "I'll begin, then. My name is Kate Stryder. This is my mate, Hugh."

"I am Talon Wolfchild, and this is my mate, Jade Callaghan," Talon spoke next, wary but willing to follow my lead.

Lucius was the first to step forward, bowing dramatically at the waist.

"I am Lucius Nicolette."

"I am Silas O'Toole," Silas stepped forward next, performing his own bow.

"And I am Augustus Lawrence," added Augustus, remaining in his spot but still bowing from the waist.

Their impeccable manners left me flabbergasted, but what Lucius said next left me speechless.

"Kate, we owe you our lives and our allegiance. From this day forward, consider us your own personal guards."

Swallowing hard, I held Hugh back as he moved aggressively forward.

Let me handle this, I told him. *We have an incredible opportunity here.*

Facing the three men, I stood and took a step toward them. Hugh moved forward with me, though remained a step behind me as I'd asked.

"Thank you for your offer, but I freed you not to be indebted to me, but to live your own lives. I'm new to the existence of

Elementals, but I do understand what you three have been through. My cousin has freed another, but she's also come up against those who were unredeemable. The fact that the three of you kept a glimmer of hope alive all this time means that I didn't do this alone. Each of you has the opportunity to remain on this path, and to live your own lives. To find your true mates."

The three exchanged glances, but it was Lucius who spoke again.

"You are a remarkable creature, Kate Stryder. We thank you for giving us our lives back, but for the time being, we would like to remain near you, offer another layer of protection."

"If that is what you are choosing, I will not argue. However, remember that each of you is free to leave at any time. You owe me nothing."

After another brief exchange, the three nodded.

Sighing with relief, I plopped back into the chair, pulling Hugh with me. He compromised by sitting on the arm rest, and I didn't argue.

"Why don't we all have a seat and chat?"

There was one long, L-shaped couch that the three chose to sit on, while Talon carefully eased himself beside Jade. She lay half across his lap, resting her head against his shoulder. I imagined his body heat did more for her than the blanket he was rearranging.

"Kate, can you explain how you helped them?" Jade asked first, her curiosity obviously bubbling over. "When I tried, I came up against their barrier."

"We apologize for that," Lucius said, directing his gaze at Jade. "We used a spell to prevent psychic abilities. That's why you were unable to reach your mate with telepathy, and why your ability didn't work."

"Why did Kate's ability work, then?" she asked.

"It must be on a different wavelength," Lucius shrugged. "It's not an exact science."

Jade looked to me, appraising. With a grin, I answered her unspoken question.

"I don't know either. But, I can try to explain how I freed them."

"By all means," Jade answered.

"I connected to them the same way I'd practiced with Hugh– basically, being able to read their souls. They were so dark," I added quietly, switching my gaze from Lucius, to Augustus, over to Silas and back. "I reached out with my own light, offering sanctuary. Each of them accepted. When I helped Silas after Lucius, I noticed that his... aura, I guess... had changed, had lightened."

"When you were helping Augustus, we could all see each other's aura's," Talon chimed in. "It was incredible. Somehow, you connected us all, not just yourself."

You took on a piece of their souls, Kate, Hugh spoke privately, anger in his tone. I knew the anger wasn't directed at me, so much, as the danger Hugh believed me to be in. *And gave them a piece of yourself.*

Which I would do again, gladly, if it means giving back their lives.

On this point I was firm, and though I sensed Hugh wanted to argue with those words, he held back.

"It is truly an exceptional gift," Lucius said, that same reverent undertone in his voice.

"Sorry I missed it," Jade smirked. "Though, I'm wondering... what can the three of you tell us about the time before you were shadowmen? Was it a gradual change, or a final decision that led you to that life? How old were you?"

Talon squeezed her arm, an amused smile on his face.

"Slow down, love," he chided gently.

Her train of thought, while seemingly random, usually had a point. I waited for the answers along with the rest of the room.

This time, Augustus spoke first. "It was a gradual change, for the three of us. You see, while we did not know each other for the first part of our lives, we became close. We hunted evil together, in all forms– human and Elemental. We've fought in wars together and cleaned up cities that were overrun by violence."

"So much carnage, over such an extended amount of time, became... disheartening," Lucius added. "When you continuously surround yourself by the evils of the world, it is difficult to remember what goodness looks like."

"We were too far down the path by the time we realized what was happening," Silas continued. "We made a pact to save the remaining goodness inside until we could find our mate, and she could restore what once was."

I let out a breath after hearing their story, my heart reaching out to the three warriors who had given- literally- heart and soul to their cause.

If I was feeling empathy for the trio, I knew Jade had to be in overdrive.

"I can't imagine the struggle you've been through," Jade murmured. "And I'm so happy Kate was able to restore you."

"Jade, you never ask anything without a purpose. What are you thinking?" I asked.

She let out a breath and sat up, wrapping an arm around Talon's neck to support herself. "Frances, the shadowman I released, was a small child when the darkness took hold. When I freed him, it was as if he reverted back to that time. He's with our friend Lani now, and she describes him like a teenager. I was wondering if all freed shadowmen would be the same, or if they would revert back to the time the darkness took hold."

"That is an interesting theory," Lucius appraised Jade with a newfound respect. "But all we have to go off of are this Frances and ourselves. I don't feel as if I'm acting like a child."

He rose a brow, and I felt my lips twitch. He'd just made a joke.

"Perhaps, with time, we'll come to a more conclusive result," Talon spoke up.

"How did you find us?" I asked of Lucius.

We'd been operating under the assumption that shadowmen couldn't sense me.

Lucius inclined his head, as if he could read my thoughts.

"The old-fashioned way," he said with a twist of his lips, as if the concept amused him. "Detective work, you might say."

After a moment of silence, Talon excused us all.

"Jade and Kate both need to rest to recoup their strength," Talon said, then turned to the former shadowmen. "You three are welcome to stay here for now, until we figure out what the future holds."

"We will look over you all," Lucius offered, standing with his friends. "We owe you that much, at the very least."

Standing, I gripped Hugh's hand and smiled at the three former shadowmen.

"Goodnight," I told them.

They all returned my sentiment, then disappeared into the night. On impulse I hugged Jade, still wrapped in her blanket.

"Rest well, Jade. We need you at full strength."

Climbing the stairs, I found the bedroom with our luggage, approaching the window to look out at the forest below. The moon was bright, and was the only light in this secluded area. I felt eyes watching, so after a brief smile into the night, I pulled the curtains closed.

Hugh was standing by the closed door, watching me as I turned. The anger still bubbled beneath the surface, and I knew we would have to deal with it before either of us could get any rest.

Before he could speak, I walked the several feet and wrapped my arms around his waist, burying my face in his chest. The move surprised him, but he wrapped his arms around my waist in response.

"Never, ever scare me like that again," he chastised softly. "You hear me, Kate? I cannot lose you. Not to shadowmen, not to your powers, and certainly not to three men who think they have a claim on you."

Muffled laughter met his statement, and I looked up at him with mirth and love shining in my eyes.

"You really think one of them could replace you? Is this jealousy I hear?"

Hugh frowned, the line creasing between his brows as he studied my face.

"No. Don't be ridiculous. I don't get jealous."

"Yes, you do. But it's all right. It's kind of cute," I told him with a playful smirk.

Stepping away, I let out a long breath.

"I could really use a long, hot shower," I told him. Then, an idea struck. "Hey, do you think you could put a sound barrier around our room? Kind of like the spells they used?"

His brows drew down, still miffed from our conversation. "I believe so, why?"

With a teasing smirk, I lifted my shirt over my head and dropped it at his feet.

"Because, you're taking the shower with me."

All traces of irritation lifted in an instant. His hands dropped to his sides, his eyes roving over my bare skin as I peeled off the grimy pants next.

Turning, I tossed a smile over my shoulder.

"Hurry with that spell," I called out, unhooking my bra as I walked to the adjoining room.

I tossed the article through the doorway as I blasted the heat of the shower. Dirt and grime covered every inch of skin, and I couldn't wait to be under the spray.

There was a light shimmer to the air, telling me that Hugh had succeeded with our private little bubble. In the same instant he was beside me, the bare skin of his chest pressing into my back.

"This is the best idea you've had all day," he whispered into my ear, circling my waist with his strong arms.

"I thought so, too," I replied, already breathless as his hands began to blaze along my skin.

We stumbled into the shower, turning until we were chest to chest, our lips meeting with a furious passion. I released all my emotions of the last 24 hours, while Hugh unleashed his terror of losing me. He pressed me against the glass, gripping my wrists in an unbreakable grip above my head.

"Tell me who your mate is," he growled against my lips.

"You are, Hugh. You're my mate," I breathed back.

Releasing my arms, he wrapped his hands around my hips, lifting me from my feet. My legs wrapped around his waist as my arms circled his neck, our lips fused together.

This wasn't slow and gentle, as our first time had been. There was a furious need flowing between us, and the more he gave, the more I took.

When he gripped my hips, I arched into him, hungry for more. When he nipped along my neck, I threw it back, begging for him to complete us.

Take what you need, I sent into his mind. *Everything I have is yours, as you are mine.*

His body took me as his teeth sank deep, joining us in the way of his people. My body spiraled out, and immediately began building the tension again. All I could do was hold on as Hugh tipped me over the edge, again and again.

Finally, he swept his tongue across the two pinpricks in my throat and lifted his head to stare directly into my eyes, straight down to my very soul.

You're mine, Kate. For now and always.

His words let loose one last tidal wave, this time taking us both along for the ride.

Chapter 20

I woke slowly, skating on the edges of a beautiful dream. My body was soft and pliant, deliciously used. A hot, strong arm wrapped around my waist and I let out a sigh of utter contentment.

"Mm, I don't want to move," I muttered lightly. "Let's stay here forever."

"Don't tempt me," was Hugh's reply.

My lips turned up at the corners as my eyes opened. Hugh's beloved face was just inches from mine, his hooded eyes watching me with an expression I recognized. An expression that made my heart beat with anticipation.

The man was insatiable. He'd carried me from the shower to the bed, only to lavish his attentions on me in a slower, gentler way. The intensity between us was no less, and I had eventually drifted off to sleep. When I woke, it was to his roaming hands, or his mouth on mine. He took me over and over again, as if he needed to assure himself I was real and in his arms.

Yes, the man was insatiable. But, then again, so was I.

Turning into him, I pressed my lips against his, igniting the fire that always seemed to burn on low. My leg hooked around his waist, aligning myself to him.

"Will it ever be enough?" I wondered aloud.

"I hope not," was the reply, before he deepened the kiss and joined our bodies together.

We moved in perfect harmony, each shuddering sigh met with a kiss, every touch only sparking the growing need deep inside both of us.

My body wound tighter, releasing with his name on my lips.

Still entwined, we sank back to the bed, allowing our hearts to return to a normal beat. I rested my head against his chest, contemplating not only our current situation, but our possible future.

"Hugh, I want to become like you," I said aloud.

There was a moment of absolute silence, before he lifted my chin with gentle fingers to meet my gaze.

"That is not something you have to decide now," he began, but I cut him off gently.

"No, I've made the decision. But, I don't want to do it now. Besides the fact that I start work in just a few days and we should plan for the conversion to take at least seven, I'm not quite ready yet."

Shifting until I was resting against an elbow, I watched his expression carefully.

"Jade and I talked about this a while ago. She had wanted to turn, but Talon was set against it. They ran out of options when she was shot. I don't want our decision to do this to be taken away, to be a last resort. I want it to be something we plan for."

"Once I get my memory back, or at least find my family," Hugh added. "That's what you wish to wait for, is it not?"

Nodding, I explained, "Yes, part of it."

"What if I don't get my memory back?" he asked quietly.

With a shrug I answered, "I'll want to do it anyway. Hugh, you are not your past, or your family. I want to be with you, no matter what. I just want to do it on my time. On *our* time."

"All right," he finally agreed, kissing me lightly.

As the kiss began to deepen, I let out a bubble of laughter.

"We better not get started again," I told him. "We'll never get out of this bed."

"And that's a problem, why?" he asked, truly perplexed.

"Crazy man. What am I going to do with you?"

His little boy smile grew into full wattage. "It looks like you're going to keep me."

Sitting up, I let out a small sigh. "Yes, along with a trio of overprotective big brothers, it seems."

"Don't remind me," Hugh groaned. "This is definitely going to get interesting."

"That it will," I smirked. "But, I truly believe they can be good again. That they can find their mates, and I want to help them."

"Do you think you feel responsible for them because you freed them, or because you carry a piece of their souls with you?" Hugh asked, studying me.

"I guess we'll never really know. But, I do know that I have to use this ability to help others. Just like Jade does."

"You two are truly remarkable," Hugh said fervently. I looked down at him, basking in the love in his expression as he added, "I love you more than my own life."

Shifting back to him, I gave in to my needs. Though I could hear tinkering in the kitchen, and I knew we had a lot to figure out with the rest of the gang, I immersed myself in Hugh.

The rest of them could wait.

∞ ∞ ∞

*A*fter another shower, I threw on a pair of jeans and a t-shirt, my usual relaxing attire. Hugh followed me down the winding stairs in a similar outfit, his hair damp and feet bare. If I looked at him too long, I would turn right around back to our room.

There were several rooms upstairs with en suite bathrooms. There was a balcony overlooking the main floor, which was one long room, allowing for two-story windows overlooking the river. The living area, where we'd gathered last night, was split from the dining area with a gorgeous double-sided fireplace.

The kitchen, where Talon was cooking and Jade was supervising, boasted top of the line appliances and a huge island, with enough bar stools to seat the four of us, plus our three guests, comfortably.

As I stepped off the stairs, I smiled widely at Jade, who was sitting on the counter watching her fiancé cook, her legs swinging freely.

Glancing at the time, I realized it was early evening, so I supposed our meal could be considered dinner.

Lucius and Augustus stood in the living room, looking freshly showered. Silas was either taking his turn in the bathroom, or standing guard.

"Good evening Lucius, Augustus," I called out on my way to the kitchen.

Freshly brewed coffee awaited me, and I went straight to it. Pouring the hot liquid into the largest mug available, I rooted in the fridge for creamer, pouring a heaping amount, before turning to study my cousin.

She was watching me with amusement, and I noticed all exhaustion from the night before was gone.

"Feeling better?" I asked.

"Oh, yes," she told me. "And Lucius has agreed to teach me some of their spells."

Talon tensed at the stove, though he didn't turn around. I spotted French toast, eggs and bacon, and my stomach rumbled.

Jade rose a teasing brow. "Work up an appetite?"

Rolling my eyes, I took a sip of coffee to hide the rising blush. Hugh wrapped his arm around my waist, leaning back against the counter.

"I'm glad to see you back to normal," he said to Jade. "What is the plan for today?"

"All I can think about is breakfast," Jade answered, pointing at the pile of bacon that had already been fried.

Talon turned with a sigh, scooping up a piece and bringing it to his mate.

"This woman is never satisfied," he acknowledged, handing her the strip.

"Only with food," Jade winked, accepting the bacon and immediately munching on the end.

Talon shook his head, and went back to flipping toast. "I thought we could-"

Before he could finish, Jade's cell phone rang out. Pulling the device from her pocket, Jade grinned.

"Oh! It's Lani, I'll put her on speaker phone."

"Jade, where are you?" a beautiful, slightly throaty voice spoke as soon as Jade accepted the call.

"We're just outside San Francisco," Jade answered. "How is everything? Where are you?"

"We stopped in Las Cruces, and I found us work. Jade, you need to come soon. I'm going to strangle him."

Jade sent me a smirk, stifling the laugh that wanted to bubble over.

"Sorry, Lani, I don't have great reception, you must be cutting out."

"Jade Callaghan, don't you dare," the other woman said sternly. "You can hear me fine."

"You're right, I can. We- uh, well, we had some setbacks, but we should be there no later than next week," Jade told her.

"Is this woman in danger? Do we need to go to her now?"

Lucius had glided into the kitchen, concern etched on his face. Jade and I both hid our smiles.

"Jade? Who was that?" came Lani's voice after a beat of silence.

"His name is Lucius. It's a long story, but we've added a few members to our group."

One brow rose above Lucius' warm blue eyes, and I could tell it had been a long time since anyone had joked around him.

"All right then," Lani said slowly. "Thank you for your concern, Lucius, but I can handle myself. If Jade would like Frances to make it past this week, she'll have to come deal with him herself."

"We'll be there soon, Lani, I promise," Jade assured her. "What job did you get?"

"An office position at a construction firm. Frances will be... a laborer," she said, amusement bubbling over. "He's livid."

"It'll be good for him," Jade said. She glanced around the room once, noting Lucius had drifted back to the living room after their brief exchange. "Hang on a sec, I'm going to take you off speaker."

Jade put the phone to her ear and walked away, to have a private conversation with her friend. I was sure the Elementals in the room could still hear her if they wished, but as Jade headed up the stairs, I wondered if she and Talon had put up some kind of shield, like Hugh had for us.

Talon flipped the last batch of toast on the plate and turned to the room.

"Breakfast is ready. You might as well start now, before Jade gets a hold of it," Talon said.

Silas came down the stairs then, his damp hair evidence of his shower. We passed around plates and just started eating when Jade returned.

"I see how it is," she grumbled, before heading to the counter to serve up her meal.

Talon beat her to it, opening the oven to reveal an over-flowing plate. "You know I would never forget about you, love."

"This is why I'm marrying you," she grinned, kissing his cheek.

Chapter 21

We gathered around the dining table, which was large enough to fit double the size of our group.

Though the trio of former shadowmen looked anything but at ease doing an activity as mundane as eating breakfast at a dining table, they pushed their way through.

"Besides wanting to strangle Frances, how is Lani?" Talon asked Jade.

"Sounds like she's found a good place to work, it's right outside the Mescalero Apache Tribe Reservation. She said it's a small company, and their main job right now happens to be on the reservation, so that should help her ingratiate herself."

"I'm excited to show you my homeland," Talon said, squeezing Jade's hand. "Though we couldn't be there right away, I'm glad Lani has found a way in."

"Where are you three from?" I asked of Lucius, Augustus and Silas.

Silas was the first to answer.

"My life began in the lands of Ireland," he paused before adding, "though it's been many years since I've walked the earth there."

"It has been a long time for us all, Silas," Lucius chimed in, clapping his friend on the shoulder. "My family heralded from Greece."

"And I am from England," Augustus explained. "Talon, I must say, this is an excellent breakfast."

"I take it you aren't used to home cooked meals," Talon responded with a raised brow.

"Lucius here isn't much of a cook," Augustus returned with a grin.

Did the former shadowman just make a joke? I choked on a laugh, triggering Augustus' gaze to land on me. The smile was still in place, lighting his light brown, almost hazel eyes. The transformation from hard, evil man to this soft expression left me breathless.

I felt Hugh shift beside me, obviously uncomfortable with me staring at another man. To his credit, he remained silent.

Switching my gaze to include all three men, I asked, "Will any of you travel home?"

There was silence as the men exchanged looks. Somehow, I felt as if I'd hit a nerve and opened my mouth to backtrack, but Lucius beat me to it.

"Perhaps one day, Kate. I do not believe any of us are prepared for that."

Jade took over, thankfully, as I had no idea what to say.

"Would you be up for some training today? Talon and I would both like to learn from you," Jade asked of Lucius.

"Of course," Lucius stood and bowed. "Whenever you're ready, milady."

Jade giggled- actually giggled- and Talon narrowed his eyes.

Standing, I offered to clean up. "You guys go, I've got this."

I can help you, Hugh sent silently.

No, go, I know you'll want to learn. I'll be fine.

Our eyes locked, and I met his lips with mine, uncaring of our audience. Before it could get too heated, I dropped from my toes and turned to the rest of the group.

"Have fun, I guess," I said, unsure of the sentiment.

"Join us when you're done," Jade offered.

Augustus and Silas gathered all the dishes together before leaving with the rest. There was plenty of uninhabited space surrounding us for them to practice magic.

Hugh planted one last lingering kiss on my mouth before joining. Left alone, I let out a breath. Though dishes were not my favorite activity, it gave me a reprieve from the supernatural to feel normal.

So much had happened over the last week that it felt like a lifetime. With a jolt, I realized it had been exactly a week ago that Hugh and I had broken into the hospital to secure him blood bags. And now- I was doing dishes while my cousin, her Elemental fiancé, my Elemental boyfriend and three former shadowmen practiced magic in the yard.

Yes, life had certainly flipped on its head in a very short span of time.

Luckily, the cabin had a working dishwasher, so I loaded the machine before finishing the pans by hand. I gazed out the window over the sink, enjoying the view of mountains and pine trees. The whole place was a gorgeously designed retreat, and I was grateful to Talon for not only owning it, but allowing us to use it.

Something I'd come to know about Talon, was that money was a means to an end, and he shared his wealth and belongings willingly. I supposed, when you lived as long as he had, money had a tendency to compile. But, what I liked about Talon, was that he hadn't allowed it to go to his head. He was still connected to nature, to the earth. It was inherent as an Elemental, but even then, we'd seen first-hand how evil can corrupt even the most well-meaning.

And, unfortunately, money- and the power that comes from it- seemed to be at the root of most evil.

Unless it was used in the way that Talon did. I'd always prided myself on living simply- I didn't need a large house, or expensive things. I liked my home to be cozy, and to use my funds for other things- like travel. With my job as a consultant, I enjoyed the freedom of making my own hours, and the paid travel time as well.

Looking to the future, Hugh and I hadn't really discussed what our living situation would entail. For the time being, I would have to accept the fact that we'd figure it out, one day at a time.

I shook away the rambling thoughts, wiped my hands on a towel and made my way outside to join the others.

alon, Jade and Hugh were spaced evenly apart, facing Silas, Lucius and Augustus, respectively. Knowing they were performing dangerous magic, I stayed well away, but watched with interest.

The air shimmered first around Talon, and I watched Silas nod in approval. Hugh was next, followed closely by Jade. Though I had no idea what they were performing, I was impressed.

The three relaxed, and I took the moment to glide closer.

"What are you working on?" I asked.

Jade answered excitedly, "A protection spell!"

Lucius, in teacher mode, began to speak. "Every spell can be boosted with the right herb or stone, but it is not always possible to carry these things with you. Talon, you are closely in tune with the earth. You are a gem caller. Have you ever asked her to supply you with the needed ingredients for your spells?"

Talon looked taken aback. "I've never thought of it like that. When I've searched for gems, the earth directs me to them, not the other way around."

"Try it. As shadowmen, the earth refused to respond to our requests, but I know it's possible. Perhaps, with time, she will learn to trust us again."

My heart broke a little at Lucius' downcast face, and we were all silent for a moment. Talon was the one to break it.

"Tell me what to do."

"Dig your hands into the earth," Lucius instructed. "Call out to her, much the same way you would when you are gem calling. Ask specifically for what you want. Picture it in your mind, and send your thoughts into the earth. Imagine what you need springing up around you."

Talon took a breath and knelt, brushing his hands along the ground reverently before digging his fingers into the earth. His eyes closed in concentration as we all watched with rapt attention.

After a pregnant pause, small shoots sprang from the dirt, surrounding Talon with their youthful buds.

My jaw dropped in awe, as did Jade's. Talon's eyes opened and he gazed around him, no less shocked than we were.

Talon ran his hands through the soft sprigs, a grin splitting his face. His dimple graced us with its appearance, and in the moment, he looked like a child discovering the world anew.

"That was incredible," he breathed, standing, surrounded by tiny rosemary bushes.

"Well done," Lucius commended.

As the men shared a smile of understanding, my heart swelled with hope for the future.

Chapter 22

*H*ugh and I will meet with my movers," I told the group on Saturday morning. "I'd like to spend the weekend unpacking. You'll all be fine here?"

"You are certain you will not need us for your protection?" Lucius asked, concern marring his tone.

"I'm sure. You guys stay here and keep practicing, I'm sure you have a lot to learn from each other."

Lucius studied me a moment before looking up to the sky and letting out a long, low whistle. I searched the sky, wondering what he was up to. After about a minute, a compact yet powerful hawk circled our group. Lucius held out an arm casually, and the hawk nose-dived, coming up at the last second to land gracefully along his forearm.

"This hawk will remain near you, yet out of sight. If you have need of me, whistle as I did."

When Lucius waited patiently, I realized he wanted me to whistle. Sucking in a breath, I did my best to mimic the sound he'd made.

The hawk instantly reacted, spreading its impressive wingspan and coming right at me. Startled, I raised my arms to protect my face, and the hawk latched onto my forearm.

With a rapidly beating heart, I lowered my arm until I was face to face with the wild creature.

"Oh," I gasped, still recovering from the fright. "Hello there. You're gorgeous, you know that?"

The hawk flicked its head back and forth, and I took that to be a yes. Chuckling, I reached out slowly with a finger to stroke along the soft feathers by its neck.

"I am able to connect to animals," Lucius explained quietly. "I can see through their eyes. If you're in need, I will be able to assist, even from afar."

My jaw dropped open, which was becoming a daily occurrence with this group.

Having no words to respond, I simply nodded my head. Lucius let out another smooth whistle, and the hawk retreated, circling above.

I watched him for several beats of time before finally turning to Hugh.

"Ready?" I asked him.

"Always," he replied, taking my hand.

We climbed into my SUV, and headed into the city. As we drove, every now and then, I'd catch glimpses of the hawk high in the sky.

"Sebastian is still with us," I announced to Hugh, as we crossed by the San Pablo Bay, looping back up toward Santa Rosa.

"Sebastian?" he asked with a raised brow.

"He's watching over us; he needs a name," I answered with a shrug.

The drive from Talon's mountain home to the condo I'd purchased just south of Santa Rosa was about a four-hour drive. The drive to my office in the city would take an hour, but avoiding the sky-high rent and traffic of the city was well worth it.

Besides, I didn't plan on needing to be at the office that often.

As we reached the block I would be living on, I shook my to-go coffee cup to find it empty. We still had 20 minutes until the movers were due to arrive, so I asked Hugh if he was up for a pit stop.

"Let me guess," he grinned, tapping the cup. "Refill?"

"Yes. And a late breakfast- once the movers get there, I'm not sure when we'll have time to eat."

There was a small coffee shop just down the street- which may have been a selling point when I'd come house hunting- and I parked along the curb. Hugh and I ordered breakfast sandwiches, along with more coffee, before taking a seat at one of the small tables by the window.

"How do you like it so far?" I asked. There was more to the question than just idle curiosity.

"Kate," Hugh said my name softly, reaching across the table to take my hand in his. "Wherever you are will be home to me."

"So, you'll stay? You'll be able to make a life here?"

"A coffee shop down the street and you by my side? I can make it work," he winked, and I let out a chuckle.

"This won't be a forever thing," I said lightly, my eyes on my sandwich. "But for now, it's a freeing schedule, and good money."

"I will need to find work also," Hugh mentioned, waiting for me to meet his eye. "Unfortunately, I have no idea what my skills are."

With a wicked grin, I answered, "Oh, I can list some."

"I'm not sure any of those will assist with the job search."

"We'll figure it out," I assured him. "You can always stay at home, cook and clean and just be waiting naked for me to come home."

"Sounds like you've thought this through," he murmured, his eyes darkening with desire.

Before we could get lost in our own little bubble, I finished off the sandwich and stood.

"We better get going."

The realtor I'd dealt with met me at the door, and I introduced the tiny woman to Hugh.

"How was your drive out?" Lacey asked as she unlocked the door. "Any trouble?"

That was a loaded question if I'd ever heard one.

"Nope, just one flat tire. Nothing we can't handle."

"I'm so glad you drove with," she said, looking to Hugh. "I was so worried for Kate to be driving so far all by herself."

"Yup, he's my big strong man," I grinned, stepping into the main room.

It was an open concept of living, dining and kitchen, with two bedrooms and two bathrooms. There was a small balcony off the living room, overlooking the valley.

The tiled floors were quite the change from what I'd grown up with in Boston, but I liked the clean look. The appliances were brand new and top of the line, and the closets were large and walk-in.

There was a gift basket on the island counter, a thoughtful touch by Lacey. As she handed over the keys and had me sign final paperwork, there was a knock at the door.

"That'll be the movers," I announced. "Hugh, would you grab it?"

He opened the door to the two men who had packed up my condo in Boston. They did a quick tour to get the layout of the house before heading back down to start unloading.

Though Hugh offered to help, they gave him a resounding no.

"It's their job," I explained to Hugh with a shrug.

Lacey left, and I began opening boxes as they were brought in.

"So, I finally get to see the real Kate," Hugh smiled, picking up a small statue of a frog holding an umbrella from a box in the living room.

"It is strange, with everything we've been through, that you haven't even seen my house," I said, unwrapping several items.

The movers had brought in the majority of the furniture, and I was filling up the bookcases in the living room.

"Where do you want me to start?" he asked.

"Bedroom and kitchen are always first," I told him. "Never mind that I'm unpacking books, they just happened to be in here before the others."

"Bedroom it is," Hugh answered. "I can put the bed together."

"That sounds terrific. Let me know if you need help," I offered, then smiled at his offended look. "Right, I forgot."

He disappeared into the room as the movers brought in the first batch of kitchen supplies. I set to work immediately, unloading all the plates, silverware, pots and pans.

Hugh appeared shortly after my second box unload, and unpacked while I chose where to store everything. It took less than two hours for the movers to be done, and I thanked them profusely before they left.

When I closed the door, I turned and found Hugh just a few feet away. He had dirt smudged on his face, shirt and jeans, and he'd never looked sexier.

"Do you need a break?" he asked.

"Yeah," I said, a little breathless. Stepping up to him, I asked, "The bedroom is done, right?"

"Yes," he answered, a little baffled by my shift in mood.

"Show me," I grinned, and he immediately caught on.

Wrapping his arms around my waist, he lifted me from my feet and used his speed to race into the room. He flung me onto the fully made bed, forcing a laugh from my lips.

Not only had Hugh put the bed together, he'd made it and unpacked the rest of the boxes that had been left. It was nice to have one room that was done, even if the items were gathered along the shelves and floor. I would rearrange the items later.

Much later.

Chapter 23

After our break, I ordered pizza and continued to unpack. Hugh moved at my pace, taking the utmost care with my possessions.

"Where should this go?" he asked, holding up a large bowl.

"You pick," I encouraged him. "I want you to feel at home here, too."

He looked around the kitchen before selecting a cupboard.

"Here," he nodded firmly. "That'll do."

Turning away to hide my smile, I kept at it until food arrived. The furniture was all covered with random items, so I plopped down on the floor and popped open the box. Hugh joined me, sporting two water bottles, and we dug in.

"I'd like to do some grocery shopping in the morning," I said around a mouthful of pizza. "At least get the basics."

"Would you be opposed to a little remodeling?" Hugh asked.

"What kind of remodeling?"

"The pantry is rather large," he explained. "If you don't think we'll need the storage, we can split it in half and have a place for storing my... special diet."

"Not a bad idea," I commended him. "I don't typically keep a large amount of food at one time— I like to shop farmer's markets and such for fresh ingredients. I'm sure Talon would help you."

Talon had made a business of remodeling, not to mention the home he had completely redone that he and Jade currently lived in.

"Perhaps we could do that tomorrow, before we fill it."

"I'll call Jade now," I said, sliding the phone from my back pocket.

While it rang, I grabbed another piece of pizza. Though I couldn't eat like my cousin, I could still give her a run for her money when I'd worked up an appetite.

"Hey, Kate," Jade answered. "How's the unpacking?"

"Good," I told her. "We're just taking a food break now. Hugh would like to build a special room— do you think Talon would be up for helping with that?"

"I'm sure," she said, then paused. "Yup, he's good with that. When do you want to do it?"

I chuckled, realizing she'd used telepathy to ask.

"Tomorrow would be great, before we fill the area. We think the pantry will be big enough to split in two."

"We'll run in tomorrow morning," she promised.

"How's everything there?" I asked, realizing that even in the short amount of time we'd been away, I'd missed the others.

"Good, we've been practicing combat today. I think Talon's been close to having an aneurism more than once, watching me fight a former shadowman. But, I'm having fun."

"That's all that matters," I grinned.   "We'll see you tomorrow."

∞ ∞ ∞

*T*alon and Jade arrived first thing in the morning. The men immediately set to work measuring and planning, while Jade helped me to unpack the little bit that was left.

"We're going to the hardware store," Hugh announced. "You'll be all right?"

His concern wasn't unwarranted- the last time Jade and I had been left alone, we'd been captured by shadowmen. Of course, that had turned out all right...

"Yes, we'll be fine. You two He-Men do your thing."

"That is the second time she's called me that, and I still have no idea what it means," Hugh complained to Talon.

With a laugh, Jade pulled out her phone, typing in He-Man, and showing the gallery of pictures that popped up to Hugh.

With a brow raised, Hugh looked to me.

"You think I have similarities with this blonde man in a speedo?"

"Let's just call it a compliment, shall we?" Talon grinned, and, after kissing Jade on the cheek, walked out the door.

Hugh followed suit, leaving me just a little breathless in the process.

Jade chuckled lightly. "They're something else, aren't they?"

"You could say that again," I grinned. Then, on a serious note, I told her, "I've decided to be converted."

"That's huge. You're sure?"

"Yes," I told her decisively. "But, not yet. We've decided to wait a little longer, but I don't want to have the choice taken from us."

"I totally get that," Jade responded, and I realized I might have put my foot in my mouth. "Don't worry, I do know how you feel."

"Thanks," I smiled at her, relieved at her ability to read and deflect emotion.

Talon and Hugh managed to finish the secret room by the end of the day. After the couple headed back to the cabin, I wrapped my arms around Hugh, looking around our cozy condo. Jade had been a madwoman, unpacking the rest of the boxes and helping to organize.

Though I slept off and on that night, I woke in the morning feeling completely refreshed. I still had one week until I officially started my new job, and enjoyed the prospect of relaxing with Hugh.

While Hugh finished in the shower I made coffee. As I poured the liquid into two mugs, a strange noise from the balcony had me investigating.

I approached slowly, unsure what the racket was. Hugh came out then, running the towel through his hair.

"What is it?" he asked.

"I'm not sure," I told him, edging closer to the door. Opening the long blinds, I let out a gasp.

"Sebastian!"

The bird was flopping around, running into the glass door over and over again. Shoving open the door, I held out an arm for the bird to perch on.

It stared intently into my eyes before letting out a strangled squawk. My heart beat racing, I turned to Hugh.

"Something's wrong," I whispered, eyes wide.

Without a second thought, he lifted me into his arms. As Sebastian flew northeast, Hugh leapt off the balcony and ran.

Squeezing my eyes tight, I huddled into Hugh, trying to make myself as little a burden as possible. Though it took us four hours to reach the cabin by car, I knew with Hugh's speed, we would be there shortly.

My brain racing through possibilities, I also latched onto mundane thoughts. Like, thank goodness we were dressed. I'd been wearing slip on shoes, and Hugh had managed to put some on before he leapt from the second story building.

I also realized I didn't have my cell phone, or any other way of communicating with Jade or the outside world.

Whatever we were about to face, it was bad enough that Lucius felt the need to warn us through Sebastian. I braced myself for the worst.

Hugh slowed, speaking into my mind. *You'll stay here.*

What? No! I'm coming with you!

Kate, please, I cannot have you in harm's way.

Don't you dare, I answered, clinging tightly. *We're in this together.*

With a frustrated groan, Hugh picked up speed. When he slowed again, I knew we were on the boundary of Talon's property.

Setting me to my feet, Hugh listened carefully.

I hear harsh breathing, Hugh told me.

Lifting me again, he wound his way to the field, where the group had been doing training. There was evidence of a battle; a lone figure lay in the clearing, still as death.

"No," I breathed, tears springing to my eyes.

Dropping to the ground beside Augustus, I quickly checked his vitals. At my touch his eyes fluttered open, a small, pained smile crossing his lips.

"Kate," he whispered before a racking cough cut off all sound.

My tear-soaked eyes looked to Hugh. "What can we do?"

"Nothing," Augustus murmured. "I deserve to die. At least, because of you, I can die a good man."

"No," I said sternly. "Take my blood. Blood will help, won't it?"

Hugh knelt beside me, tearing into his own wrist with his lengthened fangs.

"Please, take mine," he told Augustus. "It will help you heal faster."

"You would do that... for me?"

"We're brothers now," Hugh said softly. "I offer freely."

After a moment of resistance, Augustus latched onto Hugh's wrist. The wounds along his stomach were ghastly, and I pressed down on the worst of them with my bare hands to help stifle the blood.

When Augustus had his fill, Hugh lifted the man into his arms and walked toward the cabin. I was ahead of them, opening doors and pulling out blankets.

Blood, and warmth. Without a healer, it was all we could do for him.

Hugh settled Augustus onto the couch, and I piled the blankets on top. His hand gripped mine, pain etched on his face.

"You must find them," he breathed.

"Who did this to you?" I asked, tears in my voice.

"Daemons," came the chilling reply.

Chapter 24

M y gaze switched to Hugh; large, terrified eyes filled with grief. I knew he would want me to stay here- and there was a large part of me that wanted to comply- but he was safer with me. I was a shield, and I could use this ability to protect Hugh.

"Where did they go?" I asked Augustus.

"Northeast," he told me, his eyes closing.

He needed rest, and we needed to get moving.

Standing, I faced Hugh. My hands were covered in blood, so I ran to the kitchen to wash them.

"Don't even think about leaving me behind," I told him. "I can protect you. Even if it only gets you closer without being discovered, I need to be with you."

"Kate, if something happens to you... I could never live with myself."

"And you think I could, if something happened to you?"

Wiping my hands on a paper towel, I turned to face him.

"You're my mate. My cousin, my friends- my *family* is out there. We do this together."

While I spoke, I grabbed a backpack and ripped open the cupboards, searching for supplies. Talon had been stock-piling ingredients to assist with spells, and I crammed the bag full of them.

I also collected several bags of blood from his secret stash, knowing that whatever had happened to the group, they would be weak.

Hugh was still internally debating my logic, even while he assisted me with my frenzied task. When we finished, I had an idea and walked back outside.

Letting out a low whistle, I waited patiently for Sebastian to return. When he did, he was still frazzled.

"Show me to Lucius," I said to the bird. "Take us there now."

He let out a squawk before taking to the sky. Looking at Hugh, I raised a brow.

"Well? Let's go," I told him.

With a heavy sigh, Hugh lifted me into his arms. We followed the hawk through the mountainside, toward the lone peak still chilly enough to be enveloped in snow this late in June.

Caribou Mountain, one of the highest in the region. Sebastian circled and landed on a tree branch. Hugh slowed and set me to my feet as we both took a good look around.

Am I missing something? I asked him.

Only if I am, too.

Hugh concentrated, expanding his hearing. His eyes widened as he focused back on me.

They're in the mountain.

I stared at the cliff face before us, confusion momentarily befuddling my brain.

You stay here, I'll find a way in, Hugh began, but I shook my head.

We need them to come out here. You'll be an easy target in there. We need to get them out in the open.

What did you have in mind?

Grinning, I pulled the backpack around

How's your energy level? Are you up for some spells?

Hugh followed my train of thought easily.

You have a devious mind.

Do you need to feed? I said, offering my own blood. *I want you at full strength.*

As I do you, he responded. *I will be fine. After all, I've survived worse.*

Unhappy with the answer but not wanting to waste time arguing, I began to unload the small pack.

Augustus said daemons attacked. Are there actually daemons in the world, or was he using a colloquial term for shadowmen?

I don't know, Hugh answered. The frustration in his voice was palpable. *But I think we need to be ready for anything.*

When we get them out in the open, I think I should be the one to go inside and find Jade and the others. You'll have your hands full, I have a feeling.

Hugh stared into my eyes for a long moment. A wealth of emotion passed between us, and I knew the difficulty he was having in agreeing.

Let me have a pouch of sea salt, Hugh finally responded, holding out his hand.

Placing the small bag in his palm, I waited and watched as he closed his eyes, enclosing the sachet between his hands. A golden glow flared between his fingers before dulling to a soft white.

Keep this on you. It will protect you.

Nodding, I looped the small strings on the opening of the bag around my necklace. It felt warm, soothing against my skin.

We continued to sort the pouches, and Hugh began zipping away, placing the bags strategically around the mountain.

While this peak was normally a gorgeous addition to the Trinity Alps, even I could feel the evil permeating the earth itself. We were near lower Caribou Lake, the usual sparkling blue dulled to a soft brown.

Filing that information to the back of my mind, I looked back to Hugh as he returned from his final trip. Slinging the backpack over my shoulders, I allowed him to carry me to safety.

We crouched behind a large boulder as Hugh concentrated. The first explosion rocked the mountain, dirt spewing into the air. After a heavy silence, three more explosions sounded, one after another.

Poking my head around the rock, I watched as the first creatures burst from the mountain.

Shadowmen, I confirmed.

The creatures poured out of a hidden crevice, looking around in confusion. Nearly 30 creatures spread out, inspecting the damage.

Hugh let loose with three more explosions, felling half the small army. He was leading them away from the crevice, so that I could get inside.

As Hugh allowed another explosion several hundred feet away, the shadowmen instantly turned, in full attack mode.

Taking a deep breath, I stepped around the boulder- and stopped in my tracks.

Another creature emerged from the hidden tunnel, and he frightened me to my core. I stood motionless, frozen in terror.

He was huge, near to seven feet tall. His broad shoulders and muscular abs were on full display, as he wore only dark brown leather pants. There was a staff in his right hand, which reminded me of a triton.

His eyes were so dark they looked black, his chin square and ears slightly pointed.

But, what my eyes snagged on and what had me shaking in my boots, were the two long, elegant horns protruding from his head.

In an otherwise handsome face, the horns gave away his true identity.

Daemon.

Hugh yanked me down, back behind the boulder. His hand covered my mouth in an effort to keep me from talking- or screaming- or both.

What... what is that thing? I stammered into his mind. *That's what Augustus meant... but I wasn't expecting a real freaking daemon!*

Kate! Hugh called into my mind, grabbing my attention. *Breathe. You need to breathe. Calm down or we'll both get caught.*

Closing my eyes, I sucked in a breath and let it out slowly. Refocusing on Hugh, I nodded my head to show him I was calmer.

I still need to get in there, I told him.

Hugh's gaze switched between me and the scene near the opening.

I'll drive them away. Kate... be safe. Come back to me or I will tear this mountain apart coming for you.

Though we had no time, as I'd wasted enough with my freak out, I pressed my lips firmly against his. It wasn't a goodbye kiss, but a promise for more.

Hugh set off more of his pouches, causing the daemon to lose his balance. In one leap, the daemon launched himself into the fray of shadowmen, barking orders.

Carefully making my way around, I reached the small opening with a racing heart. I watched the shadowmen scrambling, taking flight to spot the intruder. Without further thought, I slipped through the crack.

The tunnel I stepped into was wide and tall, easily allowing the daemon to stand at full height. It was thankfully empty, and I moved quickly and silently down, deeper into the mountain.

The first cavern I came upon was empty, so I slid along the wall until I reached another offshoot. Listening carefully for signs of activity, I ventured down.

The whole place was eerily empty, and I wondered briefly if all the creatures had gone to the surface with the explosions. Every so often another would go off, shaking the foundation of caverns, but I took comfort in that fact.

It meant Hugh was still fighting.

As the second tunnel came to an end, it opened into several small rooms, which had been outfitted with iron bars: a prison.

Jade was in a cell by herself, while the men were grouped together. They were all awake, but appeared weak. Slowly, I stuck my head around the corner and spotted their lone guard.

It was another daemon, standing at attention, his gaze on his prisoners.

Lucius was the first to spot me, his gaze shooting to mine.

Get out, he mouthed, but I ignored him.

Found them. One daemon standing guard. Otherwise deserted, I sent to Hugh.

There was a moment of silence, where my heart was in my throat. When Hugh's reply finally came in, I was spurred into action.

They've found me. Holding them off.

What remained unsaid was clear - he needed help.

Popping into the room, I braced myself and faced the daemon.

Chapter 25

*H*i there!" I said brightly.

The daemon's mouth dropped open at my unusual entry before he sank into a crouch.

"Stop," I commanded. "Look at me."

He stared for a moment, then shook his head as if clearing it.

"You can join your friends," he snarled.

Uh-oh. My mind trick wasn't working.

"Look at me," I demanded again, pushing all the power I possessed into the single command.

Our eyes locked, and I didn't hesitate. I didn't have time to.

Opening myself up to the love I felt for Hugh, I instantly captured the daemon's attention as my aura began to glow, its bright white light still as intense even with the addition of light pink, soft green and baby blue along the edges.

For the moment I was proud of myself for how quickly I'd called upon my power... until I studied the daemon.

There was no light, no color. Not even a black haze.

The daemon had no soul.

With a feral grin, he launched himself at me. I stumbled back with a cry, waiting for the blow. His fist came down, aiming for my stomach, and I braced for impact.

The daemon flew backward, landing with a huff. Scrambling to my feet, I stared down at myself in awe.

The protection sachet. It worked.

The soft glow it had been emitting was gone, along with the heat against my skin. Single use, then. Good to know.

Taking the opportunity, I ran to the daemon's sprawled form and relieved him of the keys on his belt.

For the first time I turned to my friends, my family, and realized they were all gripping the bars, staring at me in shock. With a shrug I freed the men– figuring they could handle the daemon– and then turned to Jade.

"What– how–"

"Later," I told Jade, watching as the three men locked the daemon in the cell. Whipping the backpack around, I pulled out blood bags and passed them around. "Drink up. We'll need all the help we can get for getting out of here."

Lucius, Silas, Talon and Jade each took a bag, ripping them open and drinking as they followed me back down the tunnel. When we reached the main cavern, it was no longer empty.

Daemons were rushing through in a long line, coming from another of the offshoots and heading outside.

More are coming, I warned Hugh. *We're on our way.*

He didn't answer, and my urgency increased exponentially.

Lucius came to the front, protecting me, while Silas was at my back. Jade was next, with Talon taking up the rear.

Lucius held up a hand, signaling for us to wait. The last thing we wanted was to be locked in battle inside the mountain. When there was a break in the daemon line, he urged us forward.

We rushed down the tunnel at human pace, allowing the daemons to clear out before us. As we exited, we came upon a full-out warzone.

Hugh stood in the center of the storm, surrounded by daemons and shadowmen on the ground. He wielded swords fashioned from the earth, keeping his attackers at bay. Not only was he surrounded on all sides, but from above as well.

"Hugh," I breathed, unable to look away from the petrifying sight.

Silas and Talon immediately launched into the fray, Talon transforming into his wolf form while Silas took to the sky. Lucius gripped me in his arms and in a blink, I was well away from the fight, with Jade at my side.

"Watch over her," Lucius instructed Jade before melting into a large, winged creature that was more mythical than natural.

Jade knelt to the ground, whispering under her breath. While she may not be as good at one-on-one combat, there was still plenty she could do.

My wide eyes, damp with unshed tears, examined the scene before me. I was the weak link here, and it was beyond frustrating.

Then, a thought occurred. There *was* something I could do.

"Jade, we need to lure shadowmen over here one at a time," I said urgently. "I can try to heal them, have them join our side."

Pausing in her chant, Jade shot me a look. With a decisive nod, she set her gaze on the closest group to us. In the midst of the fighting, we had remained invisible.

That was about to change.

Standing, Jade reached out with her special gift, connecting with the closest shadowman. The creature turned, his mouth lifted in a snarl, but took a step toward us.

He inched forward at Jade's coaxing, and when he was within a few feet, I opened myself up to my gift.

Between the two of us, we held the shadowman in place, unable to resist the pull of Jade's emotional connection or the connection of our souls. I stepped closer, reaching out to the deepest ochre I'd ever seen, and spoke softly.

"Join me," I encouraged. Though I felt the rush of time, I remained calm, as if there wasn't a war just a few hundred feet away. "There is good in you, I can see it. You can be free. You can find your mate. Join me."

The light mixed with mine and imploded, sending us both sprawling back.

Jade landed beside me, instantly turning to be sure I was all right.

"Ugh," I groaned, a hand to my head. "I forgot about that part."

Allowing herself a brief chuckle, Jade stood and helped me to my feet. As we turned, we came face to face with the aftermath of the implosion.

Dozens of eyes now stared at Jade and me; hungry eyes, looking for a snack.

"Crap," I muttered, angry with myself for not thinking this through.

A daemon charged to the front of the group, coming straight for me.

"Stop!" I called out, exuding as much strength as I was able.

Though the daemon stumbled, it didn't break his forward motion. Somewhere in the back of my mind I realized the guard hadn't been a fluke- my ability didn't seem to work on these creatures.

The daemon was within striking distance, and I pulled Jade behind me. As the daemon whipped out with his claws, another figure appeared directly in front of me.

My savior crumpled to the ground, his insides spilling out.

"Lucius," I cried, falling to my knees beside him.

The daemon watched with a vicious grin, stalking us in a circle.

In that moment, a cold calm settled over me.

This was it. This was the end.

I was going to die.

My eyes lifted and locked on Hugh, who was staring back at me. Dozens of enemies stood between us.

I love you, I sent to him.

No! he screamed, out loud and in my mind, as he began to run.

Time slowed as the daemon swung, his fingers turned to claws. My eyes remained on Hugh, with Lucius' head cradled in my lap. Jade sprang forward from behind me, but it wasn't fast enough.

The claws were within inches of my face as I made my peace. At least, for a brief moment in time, I had known true happiness. I had known true love.

The air shimmered, and the daemon that had been so close a millisecond ago was suddenly sent flying backward, away from me, away from Jade, and away from a dying Lucius.

The man that appeared before me exuded pure power. His dark hair hung to his shoulders, his glittering onyx eyes glancing down at me.

"Are you all right?" he asked in a soft tone, completely belying his muscular build.

"Y-yes," I stammered, entirely bewildered.

My fascinated gaze switched from the stranger and back to Hugh, who had stopped midstride at my rescue. From the sky, a huge bird glided down, straight for Hugh.

Hugh! I called into his mind as a warning.

The bird let up on his dive just before reaching the earth, and he shimmered into a human form. An exact replica of Hugh.

My mouth dropped open as I tried to comprehend what I was seeing. Hugh's face went slack, staring at the newcomer with a mixture of confusion, hope... and recognition.

"Jared," Hugh whispered, the word echoing in his mind so that I could hear it across the field.

Only a moment had passed, the daemons and shadowmen recovering from both the implosion of light and newcomers. The man before me braced for another round of fighting, but my eyes were locked on Hugh and the man who could be none other than his twin.

In a moment of complete understanding, the brothers stepped close and gripped wrists. The air shimmered around them, glowing brightly before bursting forth. The power of the explosion shook the mountainside, knocking all evil forces to the ground.

Chapter 26

Hugh and Jared stood in the center of the destruction, the unmoving bodies of shadowmen and daemons spread out around them like a macabre starburst. All allies remained standing, staring around them in shock. Whatever force the twins had created, it had only affected those trying to do us harm.

Besides the man before me and Jared, another new figure stood among the wreckage. His blonde hair stood out easily across the distance, and the fact that he remained standing told me he was one of us.

"Please," I said aloud, my concern for Lucius. "He needs help."

The man with dark eyes turned to me once again, kneeling to inspect the man lying so still in my lap. Lucius' eyes were closed, his skin a chalky pallor. He'd lost so much blood, I wasn't certain he was even still alive.

"Help is on the way," the man assured me. Casually biting into his wrist, he placed the wound to Lucius' mouth. "I offer freely."

Lucius was too far gone to respond, so I tipped his mouth open to allow the life-saving liquid to flow in. As I watched the blood drip in, a new form shimmered into being.

It was a woman, with wild, auburn-streaked brown hair. She smiled gently at me before placing her hands about an inch above Lucius' body, running along his form.

"I'm Reya," she said softly. "I can help him."

I nodded, instinctively trusting the other woman, while I looked up to find Hugh at my side.

"Let's give them some room, Kate," he said quietly, offering his hand.

Before accepting, I looked down at Lucius, using my power for a command he needed to obey.

"You will survive this. You will fight, and you will live."

Reya and the man who had saved me from the daemon glanced at me in surprise, but I ignored their looks and reached out for Hugh. He pulled me to my feet, and I allowed his arms to wrap around my waist. Now that the fight was done, all the terror crashed down, and I sobbed into his chest.

Thank God you're okay, I blubbered into his mind. *I couldn't live without you.*

"Shh, Kate, it's all right. We're both all right."

Squeezing tighter, I opened my eyes to look around me. The man who had been giving Lucius blood stood and began directing the others.

"Gather all the bodies. They need to be burned."

"Wait!" Jade called out. "Are they still alive?"

The man looked at her oddly. "Yes. Some are badly wounded, but alive. They are just unconscious."

"We... we can save them," Jade told him. Talon arrived at her side, wrapping a protective arm around her waist. "Please, let us try."

The ground shook, and we all braced ourselves. My tears dried and I lifted my head, though I left my arms around Hugh to stabilize myself. In front of our unbelieving eyes, the ground opened around each daemon, swallowing them whole.

In another instant, the earth closed, all evidence of the daemons- or their sudden departure- completely wiped clean.

"What... what just happened?" I murmured aloud, and I wasn't the only one with the question.

We all took another moment to stare in shock. Jared was the first to speak.

"Tristan, what should we do? Do we allow the women to use their magic on the shadowmen?"

Allow? Jared might need to get knocked down a peg.

The man who saved me- Tristan- fixed his gaze on me. "That's what the explosion of light was? You were saving one?"

I nodded. "Lucius and Silas are also ones I've saved."

Silas was standing just outside our loose circle, helping the shadowman I'd saved during the fight to his feet. I realized then that the man with the blonde hair was missing.

The newly-freed shadowman watched me curiously, and I knew he was feeling the same kinship with me as Lucius, Silas and Augustus had upon waking.

"I've never heard of this before, but it is worth a shot," Tristan finally acknowledged. He looked to Jared, Talon, Hugh and Silas. "Bind them and gather them together."

The men set quickly to work, and Hugh turned to me before joining.

"You're all right?"

"Yes," I promised him. "Go."

I joined Jade, who was crouched beside Lucius. Reya was there, but her spirit was not. Her eyes were closed and already, I could see Lucius' wounds healing from the inside out.

"She's a healer," Jade whispered reverently. Her eyes met mine, then asked, "And I take it that's Hugh's brother?"

"I guess so," I breathed out, collapsing beside my cousin. Looking over to the freed shadowman, I spoke to him. "What's your name?"

"Zane. Zane Mercer."

Zane had long, dark brown hair in a braid down to his lower back. His deep green eyes watched me with an expression I recognized from the other shadowmen I'd freed.

"I'm Kate," I told him. "You're free now."

"I am indebted to you," he answered.

This again. With a tired smile, I said, "We'll have a long talk once this is over."

Reya came back to her own form, her amber eyes blinking slowly at us.

"He'll be all right," she announced.

Lucius was still unresponsive, his skin still cold.

"We need to get him somewhere to rest," I murmured, brushing a hand across his cheek. Looking back to the healer, I said, "Thank you."

"You're very welcome," she answered, swaying slightly as she rose to her feet.

Tristan was immediately at her side, keeping her from collapsing.

"You need to feed, *tau o te ate*," he murmured softly.

She looked up at him, love shining in her eyes, and I realized they were speaking privately.

"Forgive me, we have not been properly introduced," Tristan said after their telepathic conversation was done. "I am Tristan Amiri. This is my mate, Reya."

"I'm Kate Stryder," I answered him. "Thank you for saving me."

Tristan bowed, the same kind of old world elegance as Lucius, Silas and Augustus displayed.

"I'm Jade Callaghan. That's my mate, Talon Wolfchild," Jade spoke next. "I've been helping Hugh with his memory, is that his brother?"

"Yes," Tristan answered. "We've been searching for him for weeks. Jared lost contact suddenly, and believed him to be dead. We are very happy to see that is not the case."

"And, that he's found his mate," Reya added with a smile.

I swallowed once, then searched out Hugh. The work of gathering the shadowmen was almost complete, and it looked like

Talon and Silas were performing a spell to hold the creatures that were beginning to wake up.

Hugh's eyes met mine, and was next to my side in an instant. Jared joined us, and I suddenly felt nervous. This was Hugh's family, who we'd been searching for. What if he didn't like me? What if I wasn't good enough?

Hugh's light laughter rang through my mind. *Kate, he will love you. And if for some crazy reason he does not, we will live away from him.*

Was I thinking too loud again? I asked, miffed.

Yes, he responded, kissing me on the cheek. Then, aloud, he introduced me to his brother. "Jared, I'd like you to meet Kate."

"It's a pleasure," Jared said warmly, taking my hand in both of his. "And thank you, for looking after my little brother."

"Little?" Hugh asked incredulously. "Younger, better looking maybe, but not little."

Jared snorted. "Younger by three minutes, and I've never heard the end of it."

You remember, I said to Hugh privately.

I do, he answered. *Duncan. My name is Hugh Duncan. You have no idea what a relief it is.*

Pressing into his side, I watched as Talon approached.

"Perhaps we could save conversation for a different location," he suggested. "I have a home not far from here, you're all welcome."

Without further prompting, Tristan lifted Lucius into his capable arms, while Hugh scooped me into his. Talon, Jared and Silas stayed behind to deal with the group of shadowmen.

Chapter 27

hen Hugh placed me on my feet, we were in the clearing outside the cabin. Augustus' blood was still evident on the ground, and I shuddered upon seeing it. I rushed into the house, wanting to be sure he was healing properly.

He was still covered in blankets on the couch, though I noticed Jade's cell phone on the table beside him. Our group piled into the room while I went to Augustus' side.

His eyes opened, and he smiled weakly at me. "You're all right."

"I am," I answered. Looking up at Reya, whose cheeks were flushed with renewed energy, I asked, "Could you take a look at him?"

Reya nodded and approached my side. I let her do her thing, stepping back to Hugh. After watching him in the midst of enemies, I was having difficulty being away from him.

Tristan settled Lucius carefully on the floor, cushioning him with blankets and covering him to help with healing.

Outside the sliding door, I noticed the blonde man reappear, with something in his arms. Tristan greeted him, relieving him of his burden.

Two tiny pairs of eyes gazed around the room, taking in every detail. The amount of attention the two babies displayed was outstanding.

"This is Nicola and Leia," Tristan announced proudly. "Our children."

That explained where the blonde man went. He must have relieved Reya from baby duty, so that she could come help Lucius.

I stepped closer, smiling at the twins.

"Hi there," I cooed, reaching out with a finger.

I heard Jade's muffled laughter, and turned to her with a question in my eyes.

"Sorry, when you said 'hi there' it just reminded me of you confronting a daemon with the same phrase. I mean, really, was that the best you could come up with?"

"Next time I'll leave you there," I shot back, then returned to the babies.

The girl, Leia, gripped my finger tightly. When the boy reached out and touched a finger to mine, I felt my ability shudder with power. Startled, I looked up to Tristan's smiling face.

"He has the ability to strengthen others' powers," he confirmed my suspicion. "You have an incredible strength, for a human."

"Um, thank you?" I responded, eliciting a laugh from the normally stoic man.

"It is the greatest compliment, I assure you."

There was a noise against the sliding door, and I turned to see Sebastian waiting patiently to be let in.

Opening the door, I watched as the hawk flew straight to Lucius, in a supine position on the floor. Sebastian cocked his head to the side as if examining Lucius.

His eyes slid open, and a small smile graced his lips.

"Thank you, friend," Lucius murmured.

After a beat of silence, Sebastian flew back out the door, and Lucius closed his eyes to rest.

Wrapping an arm around Hugh's waist, I leaned into him for support. There was a question I wanted to ask, but didn't know if this was the best time.

Instead of asking out loud, I spoke into his mind. *What happened when you and Jared...*

I trailed off, unsure how to phrase what had happened.

Luckily, Hugh understood. *Twins are able to connect, to combine their powers. When I saw him, all my memories returned, and our telepathic link was also reestablished.*

I'm so happy for you, I smiled up at him.

We were all silent until Talon, Jared and Silas returned. Once everyone had gathered in the living room together, we stood and stared at one another. It was quite the intimidating group, and I had no idea where to begin.

"Why don't we start with introductions?" Jade asked, and I was grateful to her for taking charge.

By the couch, Reya was blinking the room back into focus. Tristan approached her, and Reya nuzzled her children before introductions began.

Tristan and Reya, with their children, Nicola and Leia. Jared, the spitting image of Hugh. Aden, the blonde-haired man who had arrived with the children. Talon and Jade. Lucius, still recovering on the floor; Augustus, in a similar position on the couch; Silas and Zane, hovering near the door.

Once those were complete, I spoke up. "So, who wants to acknowledge the daemon in the room?"

There were a few half-smiles, but Silas was the first to answer.

"Fomorians," he said. "Old Irish legends. We've... we've dealt with them before."

I looked to Zane, who was nodding his head. "They've been corrupting Elementals for centuries, creating armies of shadowmen to use for their own purposes."

That was a huge piece of information to swallow.

"They have no soul," I murmured, shuddering at the memory of the daemon guard I'd tried to connect with.

"That is accurate," Silas agreed. "They are wholly evil creatures."

"Many think that of shadowmen," Tristan chimed in.

Silas and Zane's shoulders both hunched.

"Some are," Silas responded sadly. "But most left a spark alive. *We* did."

His statement encompassed the former shadowmen in the room.

"How did you know where to find us?" I asked of Tristan and Reya, before we could spiral down this particular train of thought.

Reya was the one to answer. "We met a friend of yours in our search for Hugh. Reese Valentine."

Jade and I exchanged an amused glance.

"Why didn't you just call?" I asked.

"We did," Reya rose a brow. "Reese gave us both your numbers, but it seems you were held up with daemons. We immediately got on a plane to San Francisco after Reese told us that's where you were headed, and once we arrived, we finally had someone pick up Jade's phone."

I switched my gaze to the table beside Augustus, where Jade's phone still sat. Even in his weakened state, he'd made sure to send help.

"Kate, Jade, you believe you can help the shadowmen?" Tristan asked. When we nodded, he followed up with, "How do you do this?"

Jade cleared her throat. "I'm an empath. The first time I connected to a shadowman was by complete accident. But, I was able to find the moment he began to turn to the darkness in his memories, and free him. His name is Frances, and he's healed now."

"Talon believes I'm a shield," I added. "And I found the ability to connect my soul to another's. I first tried it with Lucius, and was able to... I guess coax him back to the light."

Tristan, Reya and Jared took the most interest in what Jade and I had revealed, exchanging looks amongst themselves.

"Our women are powerful indeed," Tristan murmured, rubbing his chin thoughtfully. "Where are the captured shadowmen now?"

Talon answered, "I have outbuildings that are secure. We've left them there."

Tristan nodded before studying both Jade and me. "When will you be ready to begin?"

Chapter 28

It took us a few days to help the shadowmen. Of the 33 that we'd captured, 25 had been saved. The remaining eight had joined the daemons willingly, leaving no piece of their goodness behind.

It broke my heart, and Jade's as well, but we had to remember that we'd saved 25 souls– and that was something to be proud of.

The men took the remaining eight away, handling them far away from our mountain retreat.

I sat with Jade in the living room, which was currently empty of people. Lucius and Augustus both had made a full recovery, and were with Silas, Zane and the other 25 former shadowmen, outside.

Reya was feeding her children upstairs, and would be joining us shortly.

Jade took a sip of tea, still recovering from our last round of healing.

"I wonder why I need recover time when you don't," Jade pondered this as she watched the group outside.

"I'm not sure," I said honestly. "In fact, I feel stronger after connecting with another soul."

"Love makes you stronger," Jade murmured, half to herself.

"What was that?" I asked, my gaze sharpening on my cousin.

"Think about it. Hatred is all consuming, whereas love can expand exponentially. When you connect your soul to others, you're tapping into the emotion of love."

That was an interesting perspective. Jade was always good at piecing things together that no one else saw.

"Empathy is different. I basically take on the other person's emotions, relieving them of sorrow or pain. That can take its toll."

"I think you're absolutely right," I told her. "Either way, I think we've both earned a reprieve."

Jade's phone rang, and she rose a brow. "Speaking of..."

She fished the phone from her pocket, then smiled as she answered.

"Hey Reese, how are..."

My eyes narrowed as I heard panic from the other line. We'd spoken to Reese after defeating the daemons, to let her know Reya and the rest had found us, but now she sounded upset.

"Well, I might have some good news. Reya is a healer," Jade told her, then there was another pause as Reese spoke, calmer now. "Do you think you could make it out here?"

Jade nodded at whatever Reese said, her eyes meeting mine.

"As soon as possible."

Reya was making her way down the stairs, and Jade waved her over. Placing the call on speaker, she told Reese to repeat what was going on.

"Something's wrong," Reese's voice came over the line. "I woke from my conversion on Sunday, felt fine for about a day, but now I've been feeling sick and weak every day."

Reya handed me her daughter, who was soundly asleep. Narrowing her eyes, Reya thought through the possibilities.

"You believe something went wrong with the conversion?"

"That's what I'm afraid of," the young woman answered.

"I would come to you, but it may be more expedient for you to come here. Would you be able to fly out today or tomorrow?" Reya asked.

"Yes, I believe so," Reese answered. "We'll charter a jet if we have to."

"Let us know your details as soon as you are able," Reya said.

"We'll talk soon," Jade assured Reese before hanging up.

The men returned then, Hugh at my side in an instant, while Talon checked on Jade.

"How are you feeling?" he asked.

"Good, except I'm worried for Reese," she answered, then explained the situation.

We will make sure the conversion is safe before attempting yours, Hugh promised.

Smiling up at him, I answered, *I know. I'm just worried for Reese as well.*

"We took a tour of Caribou Mountain, to see if any evidence of the daemons remained," Tristan announced.

"What did you find?" I asked.

"Nothing. No evidence of their time there– even the caverns were gone. The lake's color was back to blue," Talon answered.

"My grandma told me stories of Fomorians when I was little," Jade said quietly. "Monsters that came from the depths of the earth, and the sea."

"They're gone for now," Tristan said. "We will deal with them when they return."

I had a feeling Lucius, Silas and Augustus had more stories to tell, which we would find out eventually. For now, we had more immediate concerns to deal with.

Talon gazed out the window, at the group gathered there, before letting out a sigh.

"I think we need a bigger house."

Letting out a bubble of laughter, I shrugged. "There are plenty of laborers here, and plenty of acreage. Set them to work."

Talon considered it. "It's not a bad idea. We can create almost a halfway house for former shadowmen to recoup."

"More like a halfway compound," Jade answered with a raised brow. "I love it. We can supply the material, and I'm sure everyone would work together."

We all stood then, to speak to the group in the field. I still held Leia in my arms, and she stirred awake as we moved outside.

The former shadowmen were in loose groups, talking amongst themselves, but quieted as we approached.

I felt connected to every single face; I knew their very souls. It was a link that would never fully go away.

They looked back to me and Jade with the same level of intensity as the first few we'd saved. It was disconcerting, but also gave me hope.

More importantly, *they* now had hope.

Talon was our spokesperson, offering the use of his land and money. I saw many nods in the crowd, and knew that, at least for the time being, they would choose to stay.

Once everyone disbursed into groups to search the land for the best locations to build their homes, Talon gazed out across the field that was still ravaged by the mini-battle that had resulted in Augustus' injury.

He knelt to the ground, digging his hands into the earth. I backed away, not wanting Leia to be near the evil that permeated the ground. She was fully awake now, watching Talon with an intensity that belied her age.

Reya stood beside me, amusement stamped on her face. Once Talon had completed his ritual, Reya held out her hands for her daughter.

"Watch this," she grinned, and walked to the center of the field.

Tristan, Jared and Aden seemed prepared for whatever was about to happen, but the rest of us gathered close in rapt attention.

Reya set Leia on her back in the middle of the once-grassy field. Taking a step back, Reya smiled down at her daughter as we all watched curiously.

Small spring shoots began popping up around Leia, spreading out from her central location until the entire field was rejuvenated.

As flowers began forcing their way through the earth, every former shadowmen stopped to stare, completely enraptured by the little girl's exceptional ability.

"I'd forgotten what true beauty is," Zane spoke from beside me. "I think we all have."

Reaching out on instinct, I gripped his hand in mine.

"Life is full of beauty, as long as you know where to look."

Chapter 29

Talon and Jade chose to meet Reese and Dominic at the airport, to show them the way to the cabin. They flew in Friday morning, and I realized with a jolt that I would start work on Monday.

Hugh was standing with me, watching the construction underway. Most of the former shadowmen seemed relieved to have a purpose again, and occasionally one would glance my way with a hesitant smile.

You certainly have a lot of men vying for your attention, Hugh said casually into my mind.

Jealous, Batman? I asked with a hint of a laugh.

No, proud. You did this. You're an amazing woman, and I'll spend forever earning my position as your mate.

My heartbeat picked up, and I raised myself to my toes to kiss him.

Hugh. My love. My mate.

"Enough of that," said a voice so much like Hugh's.

"Shut up, Jared," I said playfully, sending Hugh's twin a smirk.

He'd been helping with the construction, and had sawdust markings along his clothes to prove it.

"What will you do now?" Hugh asked his brother. "Will you go back to New Zealand?"

"Trying to be rid of me so quickly?" Jared asked, feigning offense. "Actually, I was hoping to stick around a while. It's been a lifetime since I've spent any time in the states."

"I was thinking, we could open up a branch of Duncan, Unlimited in San Francisco," Hugh told him.

Hugh and Jared ran several businesses together, passing it on to themselves as the years went on. The whole immortal thing could be a lot to wrap my head around.

"Sounds like a great idea," Jared agreed, clapping his brother on the back.

We'd both be working, plus we had a whole compound of former shadowmen to look after. I was excited to have Jared with us– not only would I get to know my mate's only family better, but we could take all the help we could get.

I knew Jade and Talon would be leaving to join Lani sooner rather than later, and Tristan and Reya had their own lives to get back to.

When Talon and Jade arrived with Reese and Dominic, I went inside to hug them both. There was a terrible stress lining both their faces, and I hoped Reya could assist in relieving them of it.

Reese laid on the couch, Dominic at her side. Jade and I stayed for moral support, while Tristan was there for Reya's needs. The rest remained outside, helping where they were able.

"Just relax," Reya insisted. "You'll feel some warmth, that's just my spirit connecting to yours."

Reya closed her eyes, placing both palms above Reese's forehead. She moved down the length of Reese's body, stopping to hover over her stomach. Reya rested her hands gently against Reese's middle, and I could tell the moment she left her body and sent her spirit into Reese. It was only a few minutes before she blinked us back into focus.

"Well? What is it? Just tell me straight, I can handle it."

Reese gripped Dominic's hand so hard, had he been a human it would have crushed his bones.

"Reese, everything's fine. Great, in fact."

"What?" Hope blossomed on her face. "What do you mean?"

"Reese, you're pregnant."

Simultaneously, Reese and Dominic's mouths dropped open. I stifled a laugh at their thunderstruck expressions, as Jade coughed lightly next to me to do the same.

"Pregnant? But, how... I mean, I know *how*, but... pregnant?" Reese's rambling broke the silence, while Dominic seemed to be in a trance.

"I would estimate you're only a couple weeks along," Reya added.

If it was possible, Reese's eyes grew even larger.

"Two weeks..." she murmured, doing mental math. Then, the back of her hand slapped against Dominic's frozen arm as she practically shrieked. "You *knocked* me *up*! On the first freaking night!"

Jade and I couldn't hold it in anymore. We burst out laughing, and it finally snapped Dominic from his stupor.

"You would hit the father of your children?" Dominic asked, amusement slowly filtering out the shock.

"Children? Did you say *children?!*" Reese's voice rose in pitch. "Oh, God, it's twins, isn't it?"

Reya was holding back her own laughter. "It is. Would you like to know the sex?"

"Lay it on me," Reese said, exasperated.

"Both girls," Reya told her with a smile.

"Wait... two weeks along... that means..." Dominic's unfinished thought rocked us all from our mirth.

"They went through the conversion with me," Reese said in a small, frightened voice. Tears immediately welled in her eyes as she searched Reya's gaze. "How will that affect them?"

"I honestly don't know," Reya told her. "This is new territory for me. What I can say, is that they are perfectly healthy right now. The only unusual thing is that you're feeling sick so early on."

"Okay," Reese took a deep breath, clasping Dominic with one hand and laying the other protectively over her still flat stomach. "Okay, we can handle this."

"They are strong little girls. I'll keep monitoring you as long as you need," Reya assured her.

Dominic spoke up. "We will delay our trip to Europe as long as necessary."

"But, your brother..."

"Will survive without me. He will agree that this is more important."

Reese nodded, then looked around the room. "So, what's up with you guys?"

Jade and I chuckled again before filling them in on our adventure at Caribou Mountain. Dominic's gaze darkened as he stared out the window, watching the reformed men at work.

"It is not easy for me to accept these creatures have changed," Dominic said.

Reese squeezed his bicep, and his attention was immediately on her. "They deserve a second chance. What Jade and Kate have done is extraordinary."

He took a deep breath before nodding, but he said no more.

As the group began to talk more about the immediate future, I watched as Jade checked her phone and sighed.

"What is it?" I asked.

"It's... nothing. I just haven't heard back from Lani in a couple of days, and I've tried her twice this morning with no response."

Tristan's sharp voice could be heard across the room. "What did you just say?"

Jade looked at him in surprise. "I'm a little worried about my friend, she hasn't gotten back to me in a couple days..."

She trailed off as Tristan marched over to her, gripping her arm in his fist. In an instant Talon was beside Jade, pressing a hand against Tristan's chest.

Tristan immediately backed off, though the intensity of his gaze remained.

"What is her name?"

"L-Lani," Jade answered, confusion marring her features.

"Lani," Tristan breathed, his face turning slack. "Is that short for Leilani?"

"I- I honestly don't know. Why..."

With a gasp, Jade covered her mouth and stared at Tristan in a new light. I was at a loss for what was happening, but something seemed to register with Jade in that moment.

Her next statement left us all in silence.

"You're Lani's brother."

Chapter 30

ou're Lani's brother," Jade repeated. Tears formed in her eyes as she reached out to the stoic man. "Oh, I'm so happy we found you."

"What's going on?" Jared inquired, coming into the house. "Did I hear you say Lani?"

Reya nodded at him, explaining, "Jade knows her. She knows where she is."

"But she is not answering your calls," Tristan spoke tensely, his glittering obsidian eyes studying my cousin. "Where was she?"

"In New Mexico," Jade replied. "I know where she's working."

"The desert," Reya breathed, her eyes clouding over.

"It is as you saw," Tristan confirmed, crossing the room to support his mate.

"Saw? What do you mean?" I asked, as most of the room was confused.

"It's a long story, but in addition to my healing ability, I can also see possible future outcomes," Reya answered me. "It's a new gift, and one I don't quite have a handle on, I'm afraid."

"I imagine that's not something you learn to handle overnight," I mused, suddenly thankful I didn't have the burden of foreseeing the future.

"You think she's in trouble," Reese said from the couch, and all eyes turned to the mother-to-be. "You need to go to her."

Dominic opened his mouth to speak, but shut it with a look from his mate.

"Reese, I don't want to leave you in the lurch. We do know another healer, he could be here within a few days," Reya told her.

"How quickly will you be ready to leave?" Tristan asked of Jade and Talon.

"As soon as you need us to be," Jade replied. She looked to me, and I understood the question in her eyes.

"Go. We'll be fine."

She nodded, then darted up the stairs to pack.

Tristan and Reya did the same, while Jared offered to make flight arrangements.

In the flurry of activity, Augustus, Silas and Lucius came inside with Aden. Jared briefly explained the situation, and Aden darted off to pack his things.

The other three approached Hugh and me, with Jared in tow. Lucius spoke for the group.

"Aden told us of your work in shutting down the camps that are holding Elementals and humans alike. We feel partially responsible, as the shadowmen are behind these acts of cruelty. We would like to finish what you started."

Hugh studied each man in turn. "You would be doing us all a great service."

"You're welcome back here anytime," I reminded them. "I hope you consider this your home now, too."

"We do," Lucius nodded. "But we feel this is something we must do."

Hugh held out his hand, shaking each of the former shadowman's in turn.

"Thank you for everything you've done for us. You saved Kate's life," he directed this to Lucius specifically, "and you've all kept us safe."

They each gripped my hand as they left out the back, and I watched them go with no small amount of melancholy.

As I was about to ask Jared a question, Reese's panicked voice turned all our attention to her.

"Dominic! What's wrong!"

Her mate held his head in his hands, and I had an awful flashback to my first day with Hugh, when even thinking of his past had caused severe pain.

Dominic shook his head to clear it before his glazed eyes met Reese's.

"I was reaching out to Emerson, to let him know our situation," he explained. "He... he wasn't there."

Jared stepped forward, having intimate knowledge of that feeling.

"Can you explain what it felt like?"

Dominic shook his head again, not in denial but to shake out the bad feeling.

"He's still there, it's just like he's blocked. I received a sharp pain when I tried to reach out."

Clinging to Hugh's hand, I said, "That sounds like what happened when we were first captured by Lucius. They put a shielding spell around us, to block telepathy."

It was silent for a few moments before Reese sighed.

"We need to go. If he's captured- or worse- we'll never forgive ourselves."

"But the babies..."

"Are tough," she said firmly. "Hell, they made it through a conversion, they can make it to Europe."

Dominic's lips pressed together, but Reese had a point, and he knew it.

Tristan and Reya returned, and were filled in quickly.

Taking out her phone, Reya phoned Jace, the other healer she'd spoken of.

"This actually might work out better," Reya explained. "Jace is in Europe already. He can meet up with you."

Jade and Talon came down with their luggage while Reya spoke with Jace, and we all stood, watching each other.

"I'm going to miss you all," Jade broke the silence, then fell into me with a hug.

"Be safe," I whispered to her. "If you need us, we're only a call away."

Hugh and I gathered with Jared on the balcony, sending our friends and family off with waves. Tristan and Reya with their children, along with Talon, Jade and Aden were headed to New Mexico. Reese and Dominic to Romania, where Emerson, Dominic's brother, had last checked in. Lucius, Augustus and Silas were off to search for the camps, after speaking to Aden and Jared about their possible locations.

That left Hugh, Jared and me with 26 former shadowmen to reingratiate into society. Zane, along with the 25 others who had been saved, would build their new homes on this land before finding new lives.

"We've got our work cut out for us," I murmured to Hugh. "Are you ready for it?"

Pressing his lips to the back of my hand, he responded, "As long as I've got you by my side, I'm ready for anything."

Epilogue

One month later

It was a Wednesday evening, and I was packing a bag to bring with me to the cabin. The main house would be empty– Talon and Jade had returned home to Wisconsin after seeking out Lani.

Jared and Hugh had bought a building in San Francisco to start the new branch of Duncan, Unlimited, and Jared had renovated the top floor for his personal living space.

Hugh and I split our time between the condo and the cabin, where we assisted with reintroducing the reformed shadowmen into society.

It had been over a month since our encounter with the daemons, and we'd seen no evidence of them since. Though I knew they'd be back eventually, I was determined to enjoy the downtime.

With a flexible schedule at my new work, I'd cleared a week's worth of time to spend at the cabin.

Hugh came in, with a pile of mail under his arm. Upon seeing me, his eyes lit up and he pulled me into a kiss. The fire that instantly spread hadn't dimmed; if anything, it was more intense by tenfold.

I broke away to zip the bag, slinging it over my shoulder. Hugh was perusing the mail, and he handed a piece over to me with a grin.

"This one is interesting," he promised, before throwing his own clothes into a bag.

The fancy envelope gave way to a fancy invitation; pure white with embossed flowers.

You are invited to attend the union of Talon Wolfchild and Jade Callaghan.

Reading the first line, a smile grew on my face.

"They're finally tying the knot," I told Hugh. "In October."

"That's great," Hugh answered.

There was a handwritten note from Jade, which I quickly read through.

"She wants all Elementals to be there," I added. "That includes the compound."

"An Elemental reunion... in Wisconsin," Hugh said, his own smile growing. "What could go wrong?"

Done with packing, he scooped me into his arms before running to the cabin. The mode of transportation was still dizzying- and exhilarating.

Hugh slowed outside the front door, and I looked up to see Sebastian circling in the sky. Every time I saw him overhead, I knew

Lucius was checking in. Otherwise, the grounds seemed to be deserted.

Hugh entered the home with me still in his arms to find candles lit inside the main rooms.

"They're giving us space," I murmured, touched at the thoughtfulness.

"Even though this will be painful, I wanted the experience to be as pleasant as possible," Hugh explained.

Turning to him, I pressed my lips against his. Wrapping my arms around his neck, I allowed him to carry me up the stairs. He did so at human speed, laying me gently on the bed.

"You're certain?" he asked once more.

"Yes," I replied.

Before we could get too wrapped up in each other, I opened my bag and pulled out a book. Inside, a flower was pressed flat. Gently lifting it from the page, I set it on the bedside table.

"It's the flower you picked for me the day we met," I told him. "I wanted it near. I'm ready, Hugh. Make me like you."

His mouth met mine, hungry. Passion welled between us as the fire caught and held. Our clothes disappeared as we moved together in perfect harmony.

Hugh took his time exploring every inch of my body, his perusal slow and thorough. I repaid him in kind, until we could take it no more. He joined us together on a sigh, and I arched into him, lifting my head to expose my neck.

His mouth moved over my vein, feathering kisses along the sensitive skin there. When his teeth sank deep, I let out a gasp, my body winding tight.

He took his fill without letting up his pace. When he pulled away, he lengthened a nail, slitting a line along his chest.

Take what is yours, Hugh sent into my mind.

With a tentative lick, I tasted Hugh's essence for the first time. He was sweet and spicy, an addictive blend that had been made just for me.

Taking a long pull, I drank until he pulled away gently. His mouth closed over mine again, our tongues dueling as he pushed me closer and closer to the edge. I spiraled over, taking him with me as our blood mingled in my system and took hold.

The fire that had consumed us strengthened, deep in my core. The first shuddering pain racked my body in a convulsion, and only Hugh's strong arms held me in place.

I love you, I sent into his mind as the darkness threatened to take over.

As I love you, Kate. For now, and always.

With Hugh's voice in my mind, his strong arms around my waist and his taste on my tongue, I gave over to the darkness. Knowing, when I woke, I would be stronger than ever.

I would be an Elemental.

Dear Reader,

Thank you for reading *Stowaway: Book 4 of The Gifted Series*. I hope you enjoyed this fourth installment in The Gifted Series and join us in meeting the next mated pair, Lani and Samson, in their book, *Reservation*.

If you enjoyed this book, please visit Amazon to leave a review. It would only take a few moments and would help spread the word. A review would be greatly appreciated!

As always, you can keep up-to-date by "liking" me on Facebook, @anabannovels

Always, Ana

Other books by Ana Ban:

The Parker Grey Series

Abstraction; A Parker Grey Novel (Book 1)

Backfire; A Parker Grey Novel (Book 2)

Coercion; A Parker Grey Novel (Book 3)

Deception; A Parker Grey Novel (Book 4)

Dubious Endeavors; A Parker Grey Novella (Book 5)(available June 2018)

Exposed; A Parker Grey Novel (Book 6)(available December, 2018)

The Gifted Series

Allure of Home: Book 1 of The Gifted Series

Immaculate: Book 2 of The Gifted Series

Night Shift: Book 3 of The Gifted Series

Stow Away: Book 4 of The Gifted Series

Reservation: Book 5 of The Gifted Series (available March, 2019)

The Mirror Trilogy

Infiltration: Book 1 of The Mirror Trilogy

Split: Book 2 of The Mirror Trilogy

Wakening: Book 3 of The Mirror Trilogy (available September, 2018)

45020563R00146

Printed in Poland
by Amazon Fulfillment
Poland Sp. z o.o., Wrocław